25/24

James Rour.
writer. His s.
acclaim at fes
in Llanelli, live
singing for his

...d.

PARTHIAN BOOKS

The Mayor Of Aln

James Rourke

PARTHIAN BOOKS

Parthian Books
53, Colum Road,
Cardiff CF1 3EF

First published 1998
Copyright James Rourke

All rights reserved

ISBN 0 9521558 93

With thanks to the Parthian Collective

Published with financial support from the
Arts Council of Wales.

Printed and bound by ColourBooks, Dublin 13,
Ireland.

Typeset in Sabon by JW.

Cover: Peasant Wedding Feast, 1566, Peter Breughel the Elder
© Ronald Sheridan, Ancient Art and Architecture Collection.
Details from: Cockaigne, Breughel © Ancient Art and
Architecture Collection.

Cover design by Griffiths & JW.

A CIP catalogue record for this book is available from
the British Library.

'Konrad,' said the Mother
'you stay here and I will go...
be well behaved and believe
in Him, until I come back home.'

'And oh those children's voices
singing beneath the dome.'
                    Verlaine

1

Konrad could tell Flagellants had been that way recently, from the blood-trails on the road. He had walked steadily all night so as to reach Aln by midday, where he was to be interviewed for the vacant post of Schoolmaster. He did not want to be late. The buoyant, tensile spring in his step indicated a man who was seldom late.

As the sun rose, he estimated he was approximately twelve miles from his destination.

There was no mistaking the hill town of Aln, located in the remote North-Western region of the Province. It could be seen for miles around with its impregnable octagonal towers and walls that seemed to grow upward from the hill. Thick streams of ivy further obscured the divide between the natural and the honey-coloured rock. Its inhabitants were comfortable rather than prosperous, peasants, artisans and gentry, whose ancestors had contributed their skills and labour to building The City. Aln was famous for producing bricklayers not scholars. Nevertheless, Konrad had plans for its children.

The North-West was not a particularly fertile region: the soil was poor. Despite this, after days of traversing desolate gullies, and cracked sun-baked earth that nourished only goats, Konrad was cheered by the sight of the sparse greenery. On the lower slopes of the hill on which Aln was built, vines and silvery olive-trees grew tenaciously. In the surrounding plains meagre crops of maize, wheat and rye were grown with great effort. Such terrain produces a distinctive breed of person. Having to carve a straight furrow on a steeply terraced hill, or cut rock and cart it from the mountains, produces a hardness in both mind and body. Each jar of oil or cask of wine was a victory won by gruelling toil against dry stubborn soil.

At that time of year the climate was moderate. Early morning mists obscured the distant mountains and forest. In autumn, the mists would virtually hide the town, and if you didn't know otherwise you might think it had disappeared. In spring the slopes at the southern base were coloured with blue gentian and corn flowers, yet in winter it was cold enough to occasionally freeze the water of the fountain in the Square. Against such cold, solid stone houses had been built. Torrential rain might swell the spring overnight into a torrent that would sweep the vines off the terraces. Survival demanded prudence, strength and stubbornness.

The stone buildings, the cobbled sloping streets (there was hardly a level alley in the town), and the ancient parapet encircling the walls, gave Aln the appearance of a fortress. But although the architecture was sober, on Holy Days tapestries and ribbons were hung from the windows and statues garlanded with flowers and vine-leaves.

Generally, those born in Aln were hard-working, self-reliant, mean, pious, and very conservative. A particularly successful and skilled artisan might talk of buying himself a villa and a plot of land further south, in which to spend the summer months, but in reality very few who were born in Aln left it. Such time and energy as was left over from the preoccupation with food and money was spent on the dull monotonies of family life, frequenting the taverns, gossip, and the suffocatingly provincial concerns of rights and privileges. The spiritual life of Aln was as barren as its soil. Not one Saint had been born in Aln. Though the people were loyal, The City might as well have been in another country and outsiders were not welcome. This was not perhaps altogether surprising since it was believed that beyond the environs of every town was danger. No one from Aln would have considered making a journey alone. A man encountered outside the influence of the town could only be considered a thief or a madman. That is why they had lived cheek-by-jowl for countless generations, and why outbreaks of the plague were still occurring.

At that time, every region in the Province had a Governor, but these were mere titular heads, skilled administrators. Power was in the hands of the Electi. It is not known exactly how or when they became what they are today, some time before The City was built. It has been possible, however, for scholars at The City University to theorize as to the origins of the Electi by studying the many remnant cults that originated from the worship of certain aspects of the natural laws. For example, the fire cult, formed by the first person to bring fire to the Province, and therefore considered to be the only person who could make fire. This man became a so-called priest, who taught others, or allowed them to assist, thus acquiring acolytes. The cult disintegrated when fire began to be used to cook food and provide heat, thus breaking the taboo. There were many such cults in those early days, animal cults, healing cults, all wiped out by the introduction of Isa, the appointed one, a former carpenter and shepherd. It was the followers of Isa who invented the motto, 'If it is good for one, it is good for all', and it was their primitive settlement that grew into what is now known as The City. From the Holy Land they brought 'The Traditions and Teachings of Isa,' which contained the most sophisticated ideas the Province had ever known. Predecessors of the cult of Isa had purified with fire, Isa purified with water. The rituals were simple: a meal, where wine and bread were eaten as symbols of the spiritual sustenance provided by the Appointed One. It was undoubtedly these early followers of Isa who were the beginnings of a rudimentary Electi, though the formation of the hierarchy took place over many hundreds of years. First came the split into the Lesser and Greater Electi, then the Agents, the Intermediaries, and finally Governors were appointed in each region. But no one could have foreseen the hierarchy developing to the point where even the Lesser Electi did not know the identity of the Greater Electi. This was a natural development, an evolution. Very few people in the Province were capable of understanding the machinations of the Epoch - such people were chosen to be Electi, such people were qualified to interfere with the mechanism. The secret identity of the Greater Electi was not simply a craving for secrecy; they were invisible so as not to be worshiped. They were thought to be able to heal with a glance, to excel at their chosen professions, to be incapable of making mistakes, and to be working on the higher evolution of humanity.

Remnants of the early cultic practices continued alongside the cult of Isa, and in some cases intermingled with the traditional forms of worship. Flagellation, for example, was thought by its enthusiasts to be the most effective spiritual purification. Aln was one of the last remaining towns that would open its gates and give food and shelter to the procession of Flagellants who marched around the outer edges of the Province, and even here support was waning. Such was the harshness of the practice that they were not allowed to shave, bathe, change their clothes, sleep in a bed or speak to a woman. Each year the Flagellants were greeted with muted interest by some and religious fervour from others. On arriving they would make their way to the church in the Square and form a circle in front of it. They would then take off their clothes and shoes and put on skirts that reached down to their feet. Then they would beat themselves with leather scourges imbedded with iron spikes, and sing hymns in celebration of Isa's passion. If a woman or priest entered the circle the whole flagellation would be stopped and they would have to begin again. Once it happened. Each day for three days, two flagellations were performed in the Square and one in the privacy of the bedroom. Sometimes the spikes became imbedded in the flesh of the penitent and had to be wrenched out. Blood gathered in pools at their feet, and their bodies became a mass of swollen blue-black flesh. After their collapse there would be a scramble by the more devout citizens to offer them food and shelter in gratitude for their sinless lives.

Skully, whose place Konrad was determined to fill, had been removed from his post as Schoolmaster for being a bully and a heavy drinker, and for producing the singularly worst results in The City University entrance examinations - worse than any of his predecessors. Before Skully's term of employment, or reign of terror as it was later called, a small number of boys of exceptional intellect had won places to the University where, at the expense of the Province, they spent five years studying and the rest of their lives repaying the debt by teaching, preaching or at best rising to the rank of Agent or Intermediary for the Electi. But in the twelve years that Skully had been Schoolmaster, not one child had come even close to passing the examination. Finally, at the request of Mr Flagg, the Mayor of Aln, an Intermediary had been invited to the Schoolhouse. After a thorough-going examination, it was found that in Greek, Latin and prosody, the children were barely proficient, and in Logic and Mathematics they were virtually ignorant.

Despite Skully's bitter pleadings and promises of sincere reformation, he was dismissed.

'It is a matter of civic pride,' Mr Flagg had told him, then repeatedly refused his request for dialogue. Skully then turned nasty. The entreaties turned to threats.

'You'll be sorry, you pompous sack of pus,' he had screamed, banging the doors of the Council Chamber with his huge fists.

'Don't think you can get rid of me easily. No one makes a fool of Skully.' The Mayor's red face went a deeper red. Skully was a bad man. Everyone was afraid of Skully.

Konrad shielded his eyes against the sun's glare and squinted at the walled town in the distance for some moments. Even at this early hour it was shimmering in the heat and seemed to float in the air. This, and its elevation, confirmed its unrealness to him.

'My Kingdom,' he murmured to himself.

It was easy to see at a glance that Konrad was a stranger to the ordinary. He was lean and tall, over eleven cubits, and gave the impression of having a powerful, well-proportioned and sinewy body under his dusty black Scholar's garb. His close-cropped hair was grizzled, his jaw fixed in thoughtful determination. He wore a pair of small silver-rimmed spectacles that seemed oddly unnecessary on such a powerful sun-burnished face. He did not look like the usual book-worn Scholar; his body was too alert and upright. In short, he was not a peasant.

He calculated one and a half hours to be at the foot of the road that snaked upwards around the hill, and another hour to enter the town gates.

Putting down his heavy leather travelling-case, he dropped to his knees in the reddish earth, sending a lizard scurrying for cover. He put his hands together in front of his chest and bent his head in the direction of Aln. Anyone observing his demeanour would have assumed he was praying. He held this position for some time. A grasshopper leapt on his thigh; the lizard glanced out from behind a rock, then froze. Beads of sweat gathered on Konrad's forehead and he began to emit almost imperceptible grunts.

Suddenly, he looked up, and at the same moment, in a deep, clear and resonant voice said, 'Before the battle. . . I have won.'

Further along the road Konrad became aware of a familiar odour, common enough on the main road to a town, that of the rotting body of a crucified criminal. It was twenty minutes or so before the source of the sickly cloying smell came into view, almost hidden amongst a copse of aspen trees. Konrad stopped to think. He was following the main eastern road into Aln. He considered a detour for a moment. He was not a man who balked at corpses, but in this heat even the strongest stomach might empty involuntarily at the appaling stench. But he was not to be diverted, he was in good spirits, indeed he was full of unbridled energy and optimism. He increased his pace slightly. As he approached the criminal he could see at once it had been a hasty crucifixion. The main pole was a roughly stripped spruce-tree and the cross piece was too thin, a mere branch, drawn downwards like a bow by the weight of the body. He noted it was a peasant's thin, under-nourished body, livid and putrefying, blue-black from the sun. The stench was so heavy that Konrad felt it like a fine mist.

He moved closer, craning his head sideways to look at the face sunk on the chest. From the bared teeth, exposed in a disgusted grimace, it was plain that there had been no redemption at the final moment. Konrad became thoughtful. He felt nothing for the despair of the man, who had probably been a murderer, but there was a point to ponder, a thought that might be useful which his death had provided. All attempts at happiness had come to naught for him. He was dead. And worse, he was ignorant of whether he was dead or merely asleep. 'Yet you still provide value,' thought Konrad, 'as a subject of speculation for me on the mystery of death.'

Almost involuntarily, Konrad stretched out a hand and prodded the flesh of the corpse's thigh. The flesh was soft and moist. It gave and burst like an over-ripe peach. A faint smile played on Konrad's lips, not of humour but of satisfaction.

The sight of a tall stranger striding through the town gates did not go unnoticed. A group of beggars who had been sunning themselves at the inner gate were suddenly roused into action and Konrad was instantly surrounded by filthy outcasts. One of the unfortunates, who had two holes where a nose had once been, prostrated himself before the stranger.

'We give praise to the honourable gentleman and humbly request his charity,' the beggar whined in a high reedy voice.

Konrad's eyes narrowed. The beggar, fearing a well-aimed kick for payment, scuttled backwards. What happened next was not what he could have expected. Konrad bowed formally, then tossed the beggar a newly minted ri. The beggar was so shocked that he forgot to spout his stream of salutations.

'Did not Isa say, "The poor shall inherit my kingdom?" You are most fortunate, are you not?' asked Konrad.

'We are Sir,' replied the beggar, hiding the ri among his stinking rags. 'Most fortunate.'

'You have no nose, which means you were a thief. He who steals will be poor. You were poor so you stole, because you stole your good fortune drained away like dew in the sun. Do you wish to repent your sin?'

'I do, Master.'

'Do you wish to reverse your fortunes?'

'Yes, Master.'

'Then give me back the ri,' said Konrad sharply.

Konrad held out his hand, piercing the beggar with a look that made him shiver despite the sun. The beggar, with tears in his eyes, fumbled in his rags and returned the ri.

'It is not enough to repent and accept that which you have

not worked for. You must reverse the deed, you must return what you have stolen. If you do this, then within a year you shall have all the bread and money you could dream of. You have already rid yourself of pride. Now prepare the way for the Creator of Universal Peace.'

With that, Konrad strode off and disappeared into the labyrinth of narrow sunless streets, finding himself in what he took to be the artisan quarter. With his interview fast approaching, he merely noted with interest the feather-merchants, ironmongers, candle-makers, weavers' shop and their industrious apprentices.

The Market Square was very wide, dominated at either end by the Church and Council Chambers. In front of the Church was a grass square bordered by railings where animals were tethered, and a whipping-post. At the centre of the Square was a large fountain which was surrounded by peasants with their wares poured out onto the cobbles. They were selling potatoes, beans, and lettuces, or holding open baskets for inspection. Konrad stopped at the splashing fountain, glistening in the sun, to drink and wash the dust off his face. Two women were haggling over a pig.

'Thirty.'

'That's ridiculous, it's a pig, not a cow. Twenty-five.'

Typical of the region, both women were wearing the coarse vivid blue and red skirts and blouses that had been fashionable in The City many years previously. They were olive-skinned and wore their long dark hair plaited. The pig began to drop soft turds on the cobbles and the buyer bent down to examine them falling.

'Definitely not worth thirty,' she grimaced.

Konrad climbed the steps to the covered walkway that skirted the Council Chamber and entered a blue-tiled garden courtyard. After announcing his arrival to the Clerk, he was asked to wait in an ante-room with the other candidates. He had been sitting there only a few moments when his name was called and he was led to the Burghers' meeting-room. Seven Burghers sat behind a long oak table in a high-roofed, wood-panelled room. At the centre sat the Mayor wearing his gold chain of office. Konrad's footsteps echoed on the cool slate floor, taking the chair indicated at the centre of the room.

'Mr Mmmmmm- Konrad, my name is Mr Flagg, the Mayor of Aln. It is my task, along with my colleagues, to assess your suitability, or otherwise to fill the post of Schoolmaster-'

'Good afternoon, Mr Mayor,' interrupted Konrad politely.

'. . . quite so. May we begin by examining your recommendations?'

Mr Flagg was thick-set, running to fat, with a ruddy complexion and thick lips. Before acquiring jowls he had been acceptably handsome. The Flaggs had for many generations dominated the gold and jewellery business in Aln and had produced many Mayors from among their ranks. At his side sat Mr Flagg the Younger, a fair-haired young man, sensitive-looking, uncomfortably stiff in formal clothes. As a young boy he had revelled in writing poetry and holy verse plays, some of which had been performed on Saints' Days. His father, however, worried at his son's increasing introspection, fed by privilege, had forced him to join the Council as Recorder and Notary, 'to put your fanciful pen to good use'. Beside him sat Mr Bock, in charge of public works, a gaunt man with darting eyes, then Mr Bull, finance, the pot-bellied former owner of The Blue Bell. On the other side of the Mayor sat Mr Farr, Deputy Mayor, Minister of the Church and childhood friend of the Mayor, uncharitable by reputation, ascetic, dogmatic and given to sudden mood swings. Next to him was Mr Snell, Serjeant-at-Arms, cadaverous, in constant ill-health, responsible for public order. At the end was Mr Map, an ancient with snow-white hair, leathery cheeks deeply scored with wrinkles, former Mayor, function uncertain.

Konrad opened his travelling-case, took out a fat envelope from a leather wallet and handed it to the Mayor. The Mayor spread the papers in front of him and went through them very carefully one by one before handing them for inspection to the others. With each paper his eyes opened wider. Several times he uttered a 'good heavens,' and once a gasp. Nor were any of the other councillors quite able to believe what they were reading, spluttering to contain their exclamations.

The Mayor straightened his back and looked at Konrad in disbelief, in awe. 'You have taught in the best schools in The City, are fluent in Greek, Latin and Hebrew, have unimpeachable character recommendations and. . .' he coughed to lower his rising voice, 'are highly thought of by men whom I myself would be honoured to have merely. . . met.'

'No one as great as the Anointed One,' said Konrad, smiling.

'Quite,' said Mr Flagg, lowering his eyes. The others just stared. Mr Flagg the Younger was still examining the recommendations excitedly, his face glowing. With an involuntary shudder, and clearing his throat loudly as if to remind himself that he was after all only hiring a Schoolmaster, the Mayor continued.

'One wonders why a former student of The City University, a tutor to the sons of the Electi, who could at the very least acquire a Professorship or some such prestigious appointment, would want to be a Schoolmaster in Aln?'

'On the contrary, Mr Mayor, these facts should recommend me to you further. My sole desire is to dedicate my energies to the development of young minds, I care nothing for personal gain. To be quite frank, I have grown rather intolerant of The City and its emphasis on gain and privilege as the higher aims. You have no idea how fortunate you are to be away from such posturing.' Konrad's praise drew smiles from the Burghers.

'Very commendable attitude,' said Mr Bull, who had never been to The City, 'Very commendable indeed.' Mr Farr seemed less pleased with Konrad's answer and asked, 'What is your opinion of the current debate on the supposed decline in the numbers of competent teachers? How should we attract a better sort of person to the profession, by paying more perhaps?'

'If you want to produce better teachers you must produce better people. Paying them more will not necessarily make them better,' answered Konrad swiftly.

'Better people?'

'Indeed.'

'Do you mean morally?'

'Not necessarily, I mean fully developed.'

'That is a rather large task, Mr Konrad, for a would-be Schoolmaster, one perhaps better left in the hands of the Electi?'

Konrad shrugged.

'Surely that is the aim of education,' blurted out Mr Flagg the Younger and immediately flushed a deep crimson.

Konrad nodded.

'Without the key,' added Konrad, 'the door will not open, no matter how long we may discuss going through it.'

Mr Flagg the Elder, knowing his friend's predilection for debate, asked, 'Any further questions?'

'Everything seems in order,' said Mr Snell.

'Are you sure,' asked Mr Bock, a quizzical look on his face, 'that a man of your experience will be able to work successfully with the children of peasants and artisans? We are, after all, a simple people in the North-West, with simple ways, though of course-'

Konrad turned his head to one side. He was silent for some moments before answering carefully.

'You doubtless will have overlooked the most crucial aspect in all the recommendations...the results! If I am appointed, I will produce results you could never have imagined possible.'

The Mayor's eyes blinked rapidly, unable to focus on Konrad's unblinking stare.

'You seem very certain of your abilities...educationally speaking,' he stammered.

'It is not an idle boast. It is a promise. I will lead more children out of Aln than ever before.'

The Mayor shrugged, chuckled and looked around his colleagues.

'Well then,' he said weakly, unsure of how to conclude the interview. 'It is incumbent upon me to ask you if you are orthodox in your beliefs and would willingly swear on the Holy Book to pledge your loyalty?'

'I have always been a most loyal and filial subject. I think my recommendations confirm where my sympathies lie.'

The Mayor relaxed slightly at this and everyone seemed highly satisfied. The famine and drought of the recent past had produced unrest among the peasants, though mostly in the South, and the Electi had been forced to act swiftly and sternly.

'Very well, should you be offered the post you would be solely responsible for the education and moral welfare of the children and directly answerable to me. You would be paid forty ri a month, and twenty ri for an assistant whom you would appoint, and who would be directly answerable to you. Do you have anyone in mind?'

'No,' answered Konrad, 'not yet.'

'Hmmmm, that might be a problem. All those appointed by Mr Skully fled after a while.'

Konrad suddenly rose to his feet, almost knocking his chair backwards.

'When I have found accommodation I shall inform the Clerk and look forward with sincere anticipation to your decision. I respect my promise to you. No one will make a greater contribution to the future of Aln than I. Good-day, gentlemen.'

With a bow so deep his forehead almost touched the ground, he left, bringing the interview to a close.

After a short time had passed, the Burghers fell into excited discussion over this candidate. Mr Map, who had missed a great deal of the interview through deafness, tugged at Mr Snell's sleeve.

'I can't think where,' he said irritably, 'but I can't help thinking I recognize this fellow from somewhere. It's those eyes.'

'Nonsense, Mr Map,' said Mr Snell, 'it's your eyes you should be worried about.'

Konrad made a round of all the taverns in Aln, drinking a glass of wine in each one. He liked the Weavers' Arms best. It was roughly furnished with wooden tables and benches and had a low-beamed ceiling, and was in the peasant quarter. It was run by a large-breasted, middle-aged woman named Kitty, a taciturn widow who brooked no nonsense from her customers.

Konrad ordered a tankard of wine from her and said, 'I'm looking for a room to rent. I hear you have one.'

Kitty eyed him coolly.

'And who are you, then?'

'I asked you a question,' said Konrad, without menace.

She said she didn't like his sort in her tavern.

'Why?' asked Konrad.

'Always causes trouble, that's why.'

'Why?'

'Because like should stick to like, that's why.'

Konrad bought her a drink and promised to drink there every night. Then she told him the price of the room. Konrad said he would take the room but at half the price she was asking. Kitty folded her arms under her breasts and rested her elbows on the bar. It was worth every penny, she said. Konrad's smile disappeared.

'Don't play games with me, you old tart,' he whispered, leaning closer.

'Do you think I can't see that this old rat-hole is falling down around your ears? You'll take my offer and be grateful for it. And when I leave you'll be begging me to stay here for free.'

Kitty threw back her head, the flesh under her chin wobbling with laughter. 'You're a madman. I like madmen.'

She said she thought there was something familiar about him.

'Do you have any relatives in Aln?'

'All men and women are my brothers and sisters,' he said seriously.

Kitty laughed louder still.

'Oh, all right then - half. But I'll have you out if there's any trouble, I know you learned types.'

'And I know you, you old slut,' said Konrad, putting a month's rent on the bar.

'Take my cases upstairs.'

Kitty nearly choked with laughter, and she laughed for most of the night over one thing or another. She couldn't remember the last time she had laughed so loud. Later that night, a boy was sent to the Weavers' Arms with a letter for Mr Konrad.

'He's over there,' said Kitty, nodding towards the corner near the window. Konrad was sitting with his back to the open window, mid-way through another story for the locals. All eyes were on him. Konrad had been drinking with Kitty until early evening when some of the older regulars had arrived. He hadn't even troubled to inspect his room after Kitty had struggled with his travelling cases up the stairs. 'Stay out of my bedroom, you old slapper,' he had said, much to the delight of the locals. Despite the steady drinking, Konrad showed no signs of drunkenness. Kitty found herself looking at him whenever she was idle. Something about him drew her attention, something else besides his pleasingly proportioned frame. 'He looks like men are supposed to,' she thought. Konrad excused himself and turned to the boy calling his name.

'What's this?' asked one of the locals. 'He's only been in Aln a matter of hours and he's having letters delivered.'

'It's a letter from the Mayor, offering me the post of Schoolmaster.'

This produced a stunned silence from the revellers, then one laughed, thinking this another joke. Konrad asked the boy to open the envelope and prove him right.

'We have,' said the boy, 'great pleasure in offering you the post of Schoolmaster of Aln.'

A cheer went up in the tavern and there were calls for a speech.

Konrad stood up, placed a hand on his chest and said with mock modesty, 'I have only one thing I could possibly say on such an occasion...Kitty! Another round of drinks, if you please, and soup and bread, I'm starving!'

Kitty was busy serving drinks until late into the night. She couldn't remember the last time she had sweated so much or taken such a large amount of money, perhaps never. While they were waiting for the soup to arrive, a drunken carpenter took Konrad aside and whispered to him with great earnestness, 'Watch out for Skully, he's not to be messed with. He's like an animal...he is an animal.'

Konrad smiled, and said nothing.

When all the drinkers had lurched home, all agreeing that it was the best night in the Weavers' Arms that they could remember, Konrad went for a walk. All was quiet, apart from the occasional muffled shout or bark. He walked under the parapet, passed the ancient silent Civic buildings and looked down into the plain below. The moon was nearly full, the sky a deep royal-blue. He scrambled up onto the wall and sat looking at the sky for some time, until he began to feel cold, strolled once more around the Square, then went to his room.

Early next morning, Konrad collected the keys to the Schoolhouse from the Town Clerk. After throwing open the shutters he inspected every inch of his new workplace, and was not pleased. He estimated it would take days to bring order to the chaos, to dust the neglected rooms and whitewash the lime-green walls. Help, however, was at hand.

It was Konrad's second day of sweeping and wiping every surface from floor to ceiling. He was up a ladder brushing cobwebs from the rafters when he heard someone cough, politely.

'Thought I'd drop in and see how you were getting on.'

Julius Flagg looked nothing like his father. He was around twenty years of age, slight and delicate, the fruit of a second blissful marriage.

'I anticipated having to clean up Mr Skully's mess so I'm still on schedule. I shall be more than ready for the new term.'

Konrad continued dusting for a few silent moments.

'I wanted to say how wonderful it is to have a man of learning to talk to, I really am starved of stimulating conversation.'

'I'm sure you are.'

'I voted you in immediately. It's obvious you're a man of great ability and I just wanted you to know that Father - the Mayor, is very excited over your appointment... and so am I.'

Konrad descended the ladder, offering his hand for Julius to shake.

'I will try my best, Mr Flagg.'

'Oh, please call me Julius.'

'Shouldn't you be at the Council Chamber, Julius?'

Julius giggled. 'Yes, I should. To be honest, I jump at any

excuse to get out of the place.'

'You don't enjoy your work?'

Julius shrugged.

'I have to follow in Father's footsteps. The Flaggs have always been, well, very important people in Aln, in the region actually. Expect I'll be Mayor one day if Father has his way.'

'Is it not essential to follow your heart, Julius? Do what you want to do and not simply pander to the desires of others?'

For a moment it seemed Julius might cry.

'Suppose it is...Anyhow, if there is anything I can do...'

Konrad stared at the young man, causing his pale cheeks to flush deeply.

'He's an hysteric,' thought Konrad, 'highly unstable.'

'As a matter of fact I'm having some books delivered tomorrow, new books for the School I ordered in The City. I think you may find it interesting to help me sort through them?'

'Books?... of course I'd be -,' Julius checked his enthusiasm. He didn't want to appear childish to Konrad.

'I'd be delighted. Naturally it would have to be after my work at the Council Chamber but -'

'Naturally.'

A look of puzzlement came over Julius' boyish face.

'Mr Konrad, if you ordered the books in The City, that must have been some time ago, before you came to Aln.'

'Yes. That's right.'

'But...'

'I knew the post was mine before the interview took place. Indeed, before I posted off the letter of application.'

'Extraordinary.'

'Julius, I can see that you have an inquisitive mind and, if you'll permit me, I would like to instruct you in one or two principles that I have discovered through experience to be true. First, a victory is achieved in two places before a single blow is struck.'

Konrad indicated his head and his heart.

'Secondly, if there is the slightest uncertainty as to the

outcome of a venture in either of these two places then the outcome will also be naturally inconclusive. Control, therefore, of one's destiny, is dependent in this case on outside circumstances, an unseen and uncontrollable force. If one had not achieved victory inside of one first, how could one expect one's outside world to respond in the way most favourable to one? I would never have wasted my time on any endeavour that chance had also had a hand in. Life, Mr Flagg, is battle, and those who don't realize that always give up before really trying.'

Julius Flagg thought for a moment. Konrad was as he had thought, a man of unorthodox views, despite the impression he had given at the interview. Pleasure coursed through him as he recognized a kindred spirit, perhaps a Teacher?

'Mr Konrad, are we all not dependent on an unseen force, meaning The Anointed One? Is He not unseen? Would it not be heresy to consider otherwise?' Konrad's eyes narrowed.

'So we are led to believe.'

Julius felt hot, and faint. He gripped the ladder for support.

'If you will excuse me, Julius, I'm afraid I must continue to clean. I look forward to discussing such matters with you another time.'

Konrad's voice seemed a long way off. Julius, a little dazed, retreated to the door, stopped for a moment to speak, smiled and left.

The next day four crates of books and papers were delivered to the Schoolhouse. At midday, Julius Flagg, excusing himself from official business, called in at the Schoolhouse because, he told Konrad, he happened to be passing, and was soon engrossed in unpacking and ticking off books against a list. The books appeared to cover every conceivable topic. Many were ancient and in delicate condition.

'It must have taken you years to amass such a collection,' said Julius in admiration.

'Many years,' said Konrad, holding and brushing off a copy of the very rare *De Consummatione Mundi et De Antichristo*, attribution unknown. Julius used up all his allowance to buy books, but nothing he possessed contained the depth or scope of this perfectly balanced collection.

'I thought every copy of this had been burned,' said Julius breathlessly, blowing the dust off a vellum manuscript.

'It is possible to find anything hidden, it is simply a matter of knowing where to look. You are welcome to borrow anything you wish, provided you use discretion,' said Konrad distractedly.

'Oh...I...I promise to take every care, thank you ever so much, I have always wanted to, but there's so much to absorb I haven't known where to begin.'

Konrad replaced the huge brick of a book he was dusting.

'Julius, you must understand that what you know doesn't matter.'

'It doesn't?'

'No. What matters is the ability to make use of what you have learned, otherwise you will become stupid. What does it profit a man to follow a commandment if in his heart he has not come to the same conclusion himself? These books should only be used as stimuli and catalysts. The Anointed One did not wish us to be slaves to the rules of men. We must all work out our own salvation. Your experience is your power. It is very dangerous to confuse knowledge with wisdom. After all, you don't want to become a learned fool, do you?'

'No, I suppose not.'

'His commandments are rules for the sinners. It is for goodly men to search within and find the source of His intention.'

'The Holy Spirit?'

'Where else will one find it?'

'But wait -' Julius' head was beginning to swim.

'There is only one Father and He is in us,' continued Konrad, 'as in every creature and therefore...'

Julius could no longer hear him. He could see his lips moving and his arms gesticulating, but through a slow silent fog.

Konrad finally brought Julius a chair and sat him down and went to his private room for a glass of water.

'Whether my intention is realized depends on your behaviour. This difficult task can be realized not when you are mechanistically following my instructions, but penetrating my intention and making it your own,' said Konrad.

Julius blinked dumbly.

'I...I...I...'

'Don't worry about a thing,' said Konrad, 'just do as I say and you will come to understand. After all, a fly can travel a thousand miles by clinging to a horse's tail.'

Opinions of the new Schoolmaster were highly favourable. His tall, athletic body and air of authority were a stark contrast to the vulgarity of his predecessor. His social virtues and good manners delighted the Gentry, while his vulgar wit and worldly experience overpowered the peasants. All were favourable, all except one. Skully had been heard to mutter threats in The White Hart, where he spent most of his evenings drinking himself into an angry stupor. Konrad was not an Aln man, complained Skully, and all his promises would come to nothing.

'He's a pious man,' responded a bricklayer, citing the incident of the beggar at the town gate, who had since been extolling Konrad's virtues to anyone who would listen, and who had found himself a job as a dung-carrier.

'And the Mayor won't have a word said against him.'

'Ah Flagg...Flagg...' said Skully, trailing off into a growl, 'Flaaaaaaaaagg.' Skully was avoided when he was in one of these moods and left to stew in his own bitter juice. But his threats were reported secretly to Konrad in The Weavers' Arms, 'If ever you show your face in The White Hart, he said he'll make a mess of it.'

Konrad laughed coldly.

'He'll be taken care of, when the time is right,' he said.

Julius Flagg begged to excuse himself from the dinner table.

'Julius,' said Mr Flagg, 'you were delayed with Mr Konrad this morning, causing inconvenience to Mr Map who was in need of some copying, I believe?'

'That is so, Father. I apologize.'

Mr Flagg would not have mentioned it - he expected little from his son - but for the fact that he had appeared so distracted throughout dinner.

'I'm sure Mr Konrad is quite capable of making arrangements for the new term without help from you.'

'I'm sure he is, Father, it's just that - I could learn a great deal from Mr Konrad that could be useful later on in life.'

'Quite so,' said Mr Flagg, wishing to close the subject.

Julius got to his feet, bowed, and left the table. The Mayor's young wife squeezed his hand tightly.

Julius locked the door of his room and stripped naked. Prising up a loose floorboard from under an expensive rug, he took out a scourge with rusty spikes from its hiding-place. Then, unfolding a large cloth at the centre of the room, composed himself for a moment, then beat with the scourge on his back and legs, until the blood ran.

All the while he whispered, 'Wipe out my sins from before your gentle eyes, wipe out my sins from before your gentle eyes, wipe out my...'

One of the spikes was bent like a fishing hook so whatever flesh it caught it tore off. That evening Julius felt a particularly sinful rage.

When feeling sufficiently cleansed, he stood and gazed at

himself in the full-length mirror. Out of pity for the man he was, he wept bitterly.

He was reminded of his beloved Saviour.

He knelt down, naked and bloody, and prayed for many hours.

Konrad was at the Schoolhouse at dawn on the first day of term, filling ink-pots and cutting quills. The white-washed walls and removal of extraneous furniture gave the room a Spartan, studious atmosphere.

Konrad placed a piece of paper on each desk, and waited.

Nervous of what to expect, the children filed in sullenly. Konrad looked imposing to them, dressed in the silk vermilion gown of the City University. They were expecting an ordeal.

'Good morning, Ladies and Gentlemen,' said Konrad when they were seated.

The children blinked and stole glances at one another. Skully had never referred to them as anything but brats, or worse.

'For that is what I expect you to become. And welcome to your new life. Let us begin our first lesson. Please take out your lexicons.'

In one movement the children took out their lexicons and slapped them on their desks. Konrad was treading slowly along the aisle when someone's behind let off a squeak of a fart, followed by a giggle.

Konrad paced back to his desk, surveying them all carefully.

'Who farted?' he asked in a calm tone.

Silence.

'I am totally disgusted with whoever was responsible for such a pathetic effort. If there is one thing I can't stand it's timid little bottom-squeaks. I'll show you all what's what.'

In one swift movement, Konrad flipped around, lifted up his gown, and with his backside in full view, emitted a prolonged fart that resonated like the base note of a trombone. Every child was frozen with shock. Mr Konrad was definitely unlike Mr Skullÿ. All their lives they had been brought up to be deaf to parental farts, and here was the new Schoolmaster with his buttocks in the air demonstrating technique.

'Well? What do you think? It's all to do with positioning and relaxation,' continued Konrad seriously. Bracing himself, he discharged another tremendous report, which forced squeals of helpless laughter from the children.

'Above all, never force a fart, or you might expel more than you intended.'

Konrad turned around and waited for the laughter to subside.

'Nothing you will ever do can shock me. Is that clear?'

All nodded.

'No doubt you are still expecting to continue doggedly the memorization of information wholly unrelated to your lives?'

Some nodded; the majority, sensing a trap, remained silent.

'Is that what you want to do?'

No one nodded.

'Is it because it is a pre-requisite for advancement in The City that you endure such purposeless, fragmented education, or is it just because you are doing as you are told?'

A dread spread through the class. This was not what they were used to at all. Skully had never asked them questions they didn't understand.

'From this day forth, we will spend one hour on the Latin primer, one on the Greek, and the rest of the day studying Topography, Geology, Flight, Astronomy, and Humanism.'

The dread evaporated, to be replaced by excitement.

'I want to ask you questions. We are going to learn useful ideas, ideas you can put into practice in your daily life. We are going to live by the most important principle of all...Value! I am here to work for your happiness not to fill you up as one who has been previously filled up with useless knowledge.'

Konrad's voice had risen. He seemed to be growing before their eyes, filling the entire room.

'Happiness !' he thundered, 'that is, not some nebulous state of emotion, but a life engaged in the creation of value, for yourself and others - that is happiness. That is what draws us closer to the greatest creator of all!...that is -'

Konrad returned to his desk and caught the eye of each child.

'If you want to?'

With a single voice, their eyes glittering, they cheered, and shouted, 'Yes !'

Konrad quietened them, raising his arms in triumph.

'I am so glad to hear it, my children. You all have seeking minds, but that will not be enough for the accomplishment of our task, you must also have obedient tongues. I must ask each one of you to promise to keep a secret.'

There were shouts of 'Yes ! yes ! We will, we promise !'

Konrad's voice descended to a whisper.

'You must promise not to tell anyone what happens inside these walls. You must not share our secrets with outsiders, otherwise your happiness will evaporate.'

Konrad made each child hold up its hand and swear.

'The day will come when storms of opposition will rage against us. We must stand firm. But that day is a long way off yet. You must not breathe a word of what I say to others. You must pretend nothing out of the ordinary is taking place here. The results of your efforts will become self-evident. Agreed?'

The children nodded reverently.

After a long silence Konrad continued.

'Good. In front of you you will see a piece of paper, ink, and a pen. Once there was a sheet of paper which was lying asleep on a desk with some other sheets of paper. When it woke, it found itself covered with marks. A pen, dipped in black ink, had written lots of words over it.

"What have you done," cried the sheet of paper, "You've ruined me with your horrible marks. You have ruined me for eternity."

"Wait," answered the pen, "I haven't ruined you, these

marks are words. You are no longer a mere piece of paper. You are a document, a guardian of knowledge, a message."

'And indeed, some time later, a man came to tidy the desk. He collected the sheets of paper to put them on the fire. Suddenly, he noticed the sheet marked with ink. And so he threw away the other blank sheets and kept the one with the written words.

'Now I want you to use the sheet of paper in front of you to write about yourself. Tell me all about why you are different from your fellows. You have one hour. Begin.'

The children scribbled with great concentration. When the hour was up, Konrad collected the papers and placed them on his desk.

'Now,' he turned to the rows of expectant faces, 'who wants to go to Greece?'

Every hand shot up and there was a terrific noise. After a short talk on the Topography of Greece, Konrad handed out copies of the writings of Socrates.

For the first time, the children were eager to translate these mystifying marks, but translate them they did, and very well too.

Late into the night, Konrad sat at his desk and read aloud what the children had written.

'I like music. I have a cat and two sisters. My cat hates babies because they drink all his milk. I like to play my own tunes. I have a whistle that I made out of ash.'

'I don't know what to write. I love my mother but you should never love someone you don't like very much.'

'I like girls. I keep my room tidy. When I grow up I want to live in The City and grow rich.'

'When I grow up I'm going to sail away to New Jerusalem.'

'All my clothes have had other people in them.'

When Konrad had read them all he sat immobile, half-focusing his eyes at the candle on his desk. He concentrated, his shadow flickering on the wall behind.

Julius Flagg was a frequent visitor to the Schoolhouse over the ensuing weeks. Konrad began to entrust him with simple tasks. He was liked by the children and was eager to let Konrad know that he was deriving great enjoyment from their discussions after school too. He had even begun to accompany Konrad to The Weavers' Arms, which caused quite a stir at first. The regulars felt uncomfortable with the Mayor's son as a drinking companion. Before Konrad's arrival they would never have dreamed of telling a risqué joke, but after a while they were won over by the young man's friendly manner. 'He goes to the privy like the rest of us,' Konrad assured them. Business in The

Weavers' Arms was booming. The regulars took to dressing in their smart clothes and inviting friends from other taverns to drink with them and hear Konrad's endless fund of marvellous stories. Most nights the tavern was full to capacity and if Konrad was late arriving there was a hushed pall of anticipation and a great cheer when he appeared.

One night, it was suggested a drinking competition be held, to see if anyone was able to out-drink Konrad. Kitty ran back and forth to Konrad's table with jugs of wine and frothing beer and Konrad drank two glasses to everyone else's one. After some hours of steady drinking, when all the hard drinkers had tottered off to the privy to retch, and lay snoring under the tables and benches, Konrad proposed a toast, 'To the gods of wine and beer!', but not one of the company could swallow another drop. Only Kitty was sober enough to appreciate his achievement.

At The White Hart, Skully said he would call on Konrad one night, and that when he did, he would be sorry.

The White Hart stood at one end of the old bridge. It was already quite busy in the parlour when Skully arrived. He bought himself a glass of yellow cider and sat in his usual place, alone.

Bakers usually stuck to bakers, builders to builders, each craftsman believing the guild he belonged to was the best. Unfortunately, there was only one other Schoolmaster in Aln beside himself. Skully's carefully amassed savings were running low and he was telling everyone that he was not about to leave the place of his birth.

'Oh, he's all right,' said one builder to another, 'as long as he's left alone.'

That same night in The Weavers' Arms, Konrad was holding his usual court. He was in particularly good spirits, tossing off drinks stood for him and returning them with vigour. Spirits rose, and the volume of talk and laughter increased with every round.

'Tell us another about The City,' a locksmith had asked.

'I bet you saw some sights when you were a Scholar there?'

'Ah, indeed,' said Konrad from the end of his table.

'When I first went to The City it all seemed very strange - the wooden houses, the constant stream of faces I didn't recognize, the swarming noise of human activity...' Konrad was lost with his thoughts for some moments, his listeners settling back in their seats contentedly.

'You have no idea the scale of wealth walking around on people's backs, the ermine cloaks, the velvets, damask, waistcoats trimmed with squirrel fur, the silks with leopard, peacock, tiger, every design you can imagine. The women especially are fond of jewelled buttons, or silver or topaz, or pearl to ward off impure love.'

There was a rippled giggle and Trask the Weaver had his mouth open.

'The men wear the most ornate sword-belts and golden spurs, and the rush and brashness of them all, as though they are always late for work - but please don't think that I believe ostentatious display to be a good thing.'

'Oh no!' was jumbled out repeatedly.

'That is all the people of The City live for. Without wealth your life is worthless there.'

'It is an abomination!'

'But I bet you had some fun all the same,' said Trask's apprentice, and was clipped over the ear for it.

'No, you are right, I cannot deny it. I did have what you would term fun. At that time I didn't know what happiness was. I dined with friends of the Electi, attended countless guild banquets and generally lived the life of Solomon. I remember one banquet held by the Guild of Trowellers, where the food was in imitation of the Temple itself. The columns were made of large sausages, the capitals were cheese and the cornices made of sugar. In the middle was a choir desk of veal and the Holy Book was made of pastry. The singers were roast thrushes with open beaks, the sopranos were larks and pigeons were the basses.'

They had heard stories of such legendary banquets before, but no one from Aln had ever met anyone who had attended one. Respect for Konrad grew even higher.

He called for Kitty to deliver another round, stood up and bowed to his listeners.

'And now gentlemen, I'm afraid I must attend to an important matter.'

The company moaned in unison, but Konrad was not to be swayed, and they knew better than to try and argue with him. He paid for the round and was gone.

Konrad was whistling as he crossed the old bridge.

Within seconds, all was silent in the parlour of The White Hart when Konrad entered and ordered himself a glass of apple spirit. All eyes swivelled from Konrad to Skully and back again. Those sitting near Skully's table moved away. When Konrad had completed the tune he was whistling he said, 'I hear you've been wanting to say something to me?'

Skully mumbled something incoherent and straightened his back.

'If you have something to say,' continued Konrad, 'say it, if not, get out.'

Whispers of amazement spread through the room. Konrad's voice was flat, without a trace of fear, but with unequivocal menace. No one challenged Skully.

'You're in my job,' growled Skully, '...and I want it back.'

'And how do you propose to do that? Kill me?' Konrad laughed, sending a chill through all present. It was not known if Skully had actually killed anyone, but no one doubted he was capable. Skully's eyes widened and his cheeks turned a livid purple.

'We'll settle the matter in the traditional Aln way,' answered Skully, his voice different, high.

'Very well - Landlord! Two candles, if you please.'

The Landlord took two candles to Skully's table, lit them with a quivering hand and went back behind the bar. Konrad tossed back the apple spirit with one gulp, and, with a smirk on his lips, sat opposite Skully. A crowd gathered around the two men, to witness what would surely be Konrad's crushing humiliation. Both men placed their elbows at the centre of the table, then Konrad's elegant hand grasped Skully's meaty fist, the candles were adjusted and their free hands strapped to their bodies with leather belts.

For a full minute, the two men stared into each other's eyes. Then Skully snarled, 'Better call the Doctor now,' and they began.

Minutes passed with neither man moving the other's hand even a fraction. Not a word was spoken, the only sound being the crackling of the candles. Gradually, beads of sweat began to form on Skully's brow, whereas Konrad seemed not to be feeling the slightest strain, in fact a smile could still be detected on his lips.

Minutes passed, and the drinkers licked their dry lips, but none was going to move an eye from the table.

Very, very slowly, Konrad seemed to increase the pressure. Skully's hand moved almost imperceptibly towards the candle's flame. Rivulets of sweat now dribbled from Skully's face and dripped onto the table. Still there seemed no visible effort by Konrad, indeed his smile became even broader. Slowly, inexorably, Konrad moved Skully's hand closer and closer to the flame. Skully could feel the heat now, another six inches and the flesh would begin to blister. His face was contorting now, purple to blue, and he started to quiver with the strain. Then, with one sudden movement, Konrad held the back of Skully's hand over the flame. There was a tremendous cheer, but then it suddenly died down. Konrad was not letting go of Skully's hand. There was a look of panic that flitted across Skully's face, then turned to shock, to pleading terror. Two streams of tears pumped out from his eyes to mix with the pool of sweat on the table. And then he let out a terrifying scream that developed into a howl, like an animal in an abattoir.

'P...P...Please -' he spat out at the onlookers.

His hand sizzled, liquid flesh dripping onto the candle, making it splutter. His pleading eyes tried to catch one of the horrified witnesses, but all eyes were on his frying hand.

'M-m-m-make him stop,' he gasped hoarsely.

No one said a word. Everyone hated him.

When the smell of burning had pervaded the entire parlour, Konrad said, 'I win.'

He then winked at Skully, who fainted.

When Skully came round, he found himself slumped in a corner, forgotten. 'They haven't even called the Doctor,' he thought.

Konrad was laughing and joking with his new-found friends, and the drinks were lined up in front of him. They hardly noticed Skully scramble painfully to his feet, and, clutching his hand to his chest like a little bird, stagger to the door and leave.

He was finished.

That night, Konrad earned the respect of all the cowards in Aln.

As the weeks passed, a definite change came over the children. Those who had habitually concocted excuses and recurring illnesses became the first to push through the Schoolhouse door every morning, eyes shining with enthusiasm and curiosity at every lesson.

'Remarkable work, truly remarkable,' the Mayor had commented on one of his inspections. Konrad accepted the praise humbly. Every parent had remarked on the cheerfulness of the children since Konrad's arrival.

'They are keen students, fine boys and girls,' said Konrad modestly.

One lad told his mother that Konrad had told them that they were young princes and princesses, who were of utmost value to the future of Aln, that they would be the leaders of the future and must begin to behave as such. That they would create a new epoch.

'He said, "If the flower does not bloom then that flower is unhappy", and it is the same with us.'

Konrad had laughed indulgently when the boy's father had repeated these 'interesting remarks,' and brushed them off as the imaginative embellishments of a child's mind. Later that day, however, he sternly reminded his class that they were not to share any of his teachings outside the classroom.

Curiously, though less than two-thirds of their time was spent with the Latin and Greek primers that had been the case in Skully's time, their fluency was increasing almost daily. One or two of the children were even composing hexameters and hardly using their lexicons at all.

'Remarkable, truly remarkable,' said the Mayor when told.

Konrad established a routine exactly tailored to suit each child. Every afternoon a certain amount of time was spent on intellectual pursuits. Karl was taking viol lessons and making steady progress, Oskar was drawing with greater skill and proficiency, Clara had developed a passion for architectural design. His design for a sepulchre combined classical solidity with a modern awareness.

Each Friday afternoon the children were allowed to take a book of their choice from the shelves, or have a private question-and-answer session with Konrad. These sessions could be on any topic and the dialogues were becoming more and more complex and profound.

Nearly every night, Julius Flagg, who - despite his Father's misgivings - had been made Konrad's assistant Schoolmaster, would return to Konrad's room to be initiated in certain educational principles, invariably followed by a heavy drinking session in the parlour below.

Julius proved himself a very willing pupil, though progress was limited.

'Tonight,' began Konrad, lighting the lamp in his Spartan room, 'we are going to study my thoughts on value in a little more depth.'

Julius looked a little downcast. Konrad had been patient with him, but he did find that theory particularly elusive.

'Tell me, how would you define true value?'

'True value is the process whereby a person is capable of deciding for themselves what is gain or loss,' Julius repeated confidently but mechanically.

'Hmm,' Konrad had never once lost his temper since being in Aln.

'The conditions for me losing my temper with Julius are perfect tonight,' he thought.

'When we say something is of little value, what do we mean exactly?'

Julius glanced up at the shadows flickering on the ceiling, and felt himself shrink inside.

'Umm.'

'We mean it cannot be considered to be favourable to the maintenance of human existence. There is no such thing as non-value, but there does not exist anti-value. Now continue.'

'Umm.'

Konrad waited for a sufficient length of time to let Julius know he was not happy, before continuing.

'While anti-value cannot be considered good, gainful or beautiful, it cannot be called non-value because an influence is still exerted on the subject.'

Julius scuffed his shoes along the floorboards like a schoolboy. He was close to tears.

'I'm a learned fool,' he thought.

'Julius, look at me,' said Konrad firmly, holding him in a strict but compassionate gaze.

'We are engaged in a most important task. More vital to the future of Aln than you can at present imagine. We are displacing abhorrent Platonic values of truth, goodness and beauty, on which our society is founded, and substituting value in place of truth...Why?'

'I don't know,' Julius blurted out, a little petulantly.

'Because truth cannot be created, Julius.' Konrad's voice was beginning to tremble. Julius' eyes were filling with tears, but also with love and awe at the greatness of his master.

Konrad opened the window and looked up at the night sky. He searched his mind for a way to make his pupil grasp what was in his heart.

'There is a difference between intelligence and wisdom,' he thought.

Calling Julius to the window, he asked him quietly, 'What is that?'

'The moon?' answered Julius doubtfully.

'Correct, and truth would say, "That is the moon," whereas value would say, "The moon is beautiful, it gives light."

Morality is relative, value is not. Truth cannot create value, value can create truth...Do you understand?'

'Sometimes, I feel without knowing, I feel more than I understand what you are trying to teach me.'

Konrad sighed heavily. 'Julius, this is my life's task. The development of people who possess the ability to distinguish between truth and beauty, and thereby create harmonious balance - will you help me?'

'I will devote all the energy I possess, all of it.'

'This is all you need do. Concentrate on this one principle. Ponder it night and day. When you have mastered it, and only then, we will move to the next stage. Do you agree?'

'Wholeheartedly, sir.'

'I know you will win through, Julius,' said Konrad warmly.

Bending his frame so that his aquiline nose was within an inch of Julius' snub one, Konrad whispered, 'The entire future of the Province depends on it.'

11

That night the temperature dropped. By morning there was a foot of snow on the ground.

'Will you be needing me for anything else, sir?' enquired Kitty after taking away Konrad's breakfast tray and bringing him another pot of coffee.

'No, that will be all,' he said, as Kitty backed dutifully out of the door. While dipping cake into his coffee, Konrad noticed what a state of disrepair his shoes were in.

'I think I can afford a trip to the shoemakers,' he said pensively.

Flaig the Shoemaker was the best in Aln, and the oldest. He kept to himself, was never seen in the taverns and was considered pious. As a young man it had been different, but that was before tragedy had struck. While still an apprentice, he had married the beautiful Nest, daughter of his master. At first they had been very happy, but then after the birth of their son, Flaig had become restless. He spent more and more time in the taverns, and less and less with his wife and son. Nest became melancholic and bitter rows ensued, which served to abet Flaig's negligence. When finally news reached Nest that Flaig had taken a mistress, in the Western Quarter - Kitty, the present owner of The Weavers' Arms - she broke. She left early one morning, with the child still in swaddling clothes in her arms, and jumped off the town wall. Miraculously, the fall was broken by a tree and they were rescued. Nest escaped with minor injuries and the baby was completely unharmed. Nest, by now deranged, was locked up in the dungeon beneath the Council Chamber, where she died several years later. Flaig, unable to speak from grief and guilt, could not even look at his baby son, so the child was sent to an orphanage in The City.

Flaig eventually recovered his voice, but never mentioned the tragedy, and never once enquired after his son. He attended church regularly, worked assiduously at his craft, and became the best shoemaker in Aln.

Konrad stooped low to enter Flaig's workshop on his way to the Schoolhouse. Flaig put down his hammer and nodded at Konrad.

'I'm in need of a new pair of shoes,' said Konrad, looking down at his scuffed misshapen shoes.

Flaig nodded in agreement.

'Nothing too ostentatious for a Schoolmaster. Just a simple pair of shoes, but stout and made to last.'

'What colour?' asked Flaig tonelessly.

'Black, of course,' said Konrad.

Flaig shrugged. A simple job for a man of his skills. He scrutinized Konrad's feet for a moment, making some marks on the bench with a piece of chalk. Such was the mastery of his craft he no longer took measurements.

'I'll pay in advance for the work, if that's all right with you.'

'If you want,' said Flaig distractedly. His frugality and constant commissions had made him indifferent to profit.

Konrad took one hundred ri from his pocket and counted the coins out on the bench. Flaig's brow furrowed. Even the most expensive pair of shoes cost no more than fifteen ri.

'Too much,' said Flaig, 'only need eight.'

Konrad's face quickly flushed red. In a voice barely containing a powerful fury, he said, 'I'll... pay... what... I... want... to... pay.'

Flaig shrugged and grabbed at his straggly white beard. Konrad left.

Flaig stood thoughtfully looking at the hundred ri for some time, before picking up his hammer and resuming his work.

12

The children had snow fights on their way to school and were boisterous throughout the morning.

'Ladies and Gentlemen,' intoned Konrad, having to raise his voice more than was usual, 'this afternoon we will receive a visitor, namely, Mr Map. I want you to behave impeccably.'

The most important festival of the year was fast approaching - New Year's Day Celebration, a three-day Holy Day. Every child and adult would be required to visit the Church on the first day of the year. They would hear a sermon given by Mr Map, kiss the Holy Book and then make The Donation. It was customary for Mr Map to visit every workplace in Aln during the weeks before The Donation, hence his impending visit to the Schoolhouse. It was his task, carried out with considerable relish, to remind and encourage the populace of the significance, indeed the honour, of being able to give as much money as their conscience urged them to, towards the re-building of New Jerusalem. Their hard-earned money would pay towards the upkeep of the Great Temple, the repair of roads and buildings, and constant recitations from the Holy Book. It was every child's dream to visit New Jerusalem one day, but few had made the journey. However, progress reports were issued regularly by the Electi. It was unheard of not to donate, no one had ever even fantasized about the possibility of not making a donation. It was too great an opportunity to miss.

Huddled in an overcoat and scarf, Mr Farr stumbled across the Square on his way to the Council Chamber, anxious to speak to the Mayor privately before the morning session began. To his dismay he saw Gammy, an idiot, smashing ice in the fountain with a stick. Gammy, who was very fond of Mr Farr, and proud of his attentions, seeing him approach, ran towards him playfully. Unable to avoid him, Mr Farr huddled deeper into his overcoat and kept his eyes fixed on the Council Chamber.

'Mr Farr, Mr Farr,' cried Gammy in a sing-song voice.

'Shit !' muttered Mr Farr into his scarf.

Mr Farr had for some weeks been in a bad mood. He'd been irritable with every member of his staff and household. He had been pre-occupied with a trying problem, and had been writing and re-writing a letter that he never posted.

'Mr Farr, I want to ask you something,' said Gammy, smiling with genuine warmth and affection, and feeling in Mr Farr's pocket for a hand that on this occasion remained firmly in its place.

Gammy was not a child and not an adult. In fact, it was difficult to tell exactly how old he was; he didn't know himself. He had been born with one leg shorter than the other, to an elderly prostitute. Something went wrong in the delivery, he got stuck, and had to be yanked out by the leg. His head was an odd shape too. Because of his good nature people gave him errands to do and he was able to survive and had made a bolt-hole for himself in one of the disused storerooms in the east wall. Sometimes, usually wintertime, he would disappear for weeks on end; no one asked him where he went, because they didn't expect a sensible answer.

'I expect you're excited at the snow, Gammy,' said Mr Farr, determined not to slacken his pace and stumbling all the more.

'Mr Farr, I want to ask you something,' sang Gammy, able to keep up more easily in his bare feet.

'Not now, Gammy, another time.'

'Why is the moon more useful than the sun, Mr Farr?'

'Haven't got the time, Gammy,' growled Mr Farr.

'Mr -'.

Mr Farr stopped and, grabbing Gammy's thin arm, squeezed it until he yelped. 'Not now - understand?'

Gammy skipped away, with tears in his eyes, back to the fountain.

'What's the matter?' asked the Mayor, as Farr pounced on him as soon as he entered the Chambers, and ushered him into his office. 'We've a lot to get through this morning.'

'Flagg, I think we made a big mistake,' said Mr Farr, as though agreeing with him.

'What do you mean?'

'In appointing this fellow Konrad.'

'Konrad?' muttered the Mayor in astonishment, 'but he's doing wonderfully well.'

'Too wonderfully.'

'What are you talking about?'

'Look Flagg, you're the Mayor, you must keep in touch with what's going on, this fellow - well, he's becoming popular, extremely popular.'

'So?' said the Mayor irritably.

'It means that his opinions carry weight with the peasants, half of whom he seems to be bosom pals with, and the other half doff their caps to him, and if he put it about that he disapproved of an unpopular measure that we might pass, well, it could go against us.'

'What dreadful nonsense this is, Farr! You're looking for enemies where there are none. If you don't like him then say so.'

'It's not a question of like or dislike, though as it happens I don't, it's a matter of stability. There's something sinister about Konrad!'

'There's nothing wrong with Konrad,' said the Mayor, making to leave, 'and we are very lucky to have found him.'

'We didn't find him, he found us, and what about your son?'

Flagg winced. His son had always been a painful disappointment.

'Do you think it is acceptable that people witness your only son spending more time with a Schoolmaster, in a tavern, than with his own Father - a Flagg!'

This last remark made the Mayor vigorously flick imaginary dust from his shoulders, which was his way of ending a difficult conversation with his old friend.

'As you rightly point out, Mr Farr, I am the Mayor of Aln, and I say nothing but good has come from Konrad's appointment.'

'I've given you a warning - put him in his place, Mr Mayor!'

'As you are aware,' said Mr Map to the attentive children, 'it is a well-known fact that the most prosperous citizens in the Province became so by virtue of the large donations they have made since they were children like yourselves. The quickest way, therefore, for the poor to become wealthy is to give what you can - what your greedy mind is telling you you can afford - and then...' Mr Map tapped his expanded chest - 'give a little more. If it doesn't hurt, as the saying goes, then it probably isn't enough.'

Konrad, standing behind Mr Map at a respectful distance, indicated to the children that they should nod.

'That's better, chuckled Mr Map, 'after all, you do want to be wealthy, don't you?'

'Yes, Mr Map,' they chorused.

On the day of The Donation, the inhabitants of every town in the Province filed into the Church and slipped their envelopes into large, locked iron boxes. Each donation, that is the amount, was given anonymously, but attendance at the ceremony was duly noted in the Church register by an acolyte. Each box was then collected by Agents from The City and transported. After the service of thanks, the local boxes were blessed, and shipped to New Jerusalem. After Mr Map had left, the children heaved a huge sigh of relief. They had succeeded in putting on a good show. Mr Map's views entirely contradicted Konrad's teachings on the meaning and significance of money and its contribution. But rather than praising his pupils, Konrad grew pensive, distracted. He cancelled the question and answer session and asked the children to read quietly. Julius came as usual, but Konrad informed him he would not be needed that afternoon and there would be no instruction that evening. Julius was disappointed; he was making progress, but accepted his master's wish unthinkingly.

'I must reflect,' Konrad had said, 'go home and rest.'

On Monday morning the sun was shining, and Konrad was more ebullient than ever. He entered the Schoolhouse smiling broadly, with Julius at his side, who also seemed full of high spirits.

Konrad's moods and teachings were growing ever stranger.

'This morning's lesson will concern a subject particularly close to my heart, namely the three most important treasures in the world. But first I must tell you how pleased I am. Your progress has been splendid and steady. That is not, however, a cause for pride and complacency. I warn you now. Next year will be even harder, but the time is fast approaching when you must teach others. Almost, but not quite...'

The children's faces were filled with a dignity far beyond their years. They gazed up at Konrad with profound respect.

'And this afternoon, as a treat, we'll make paper birds, and fly them from the parapet.'

The children cheered, beside themselves with joy.

'But first - the work!'

13

'Come in,' said Mr Flagg the Elder.

He was warming his back against the fire in his private chamber.

On the table was a silver tureen of hot buttered wine, and a plate of cakes. Earlier that week he had requested an informal meeting with Konrad, 'an informal occasion, in part to thank you for your sterling work, also to discuss future plans,' the note had said. And in part to regain the upper hand. After his talk with Mr Farr the Mayor had begun to have his doubts. It was true there was a certain strangeness about Konrad, and he was aloof. It was his intention, over a few glasses, to get to know Konrad better, find out more about him. After all, as Mr Farr had pointed out, he was not an Aln man. Apart from official administration and enquiries as to the children's progress, they had never met socially. And he had heard stories, jealous rumours no doubt, but even so, Konrad was a bit of an enigma. Even his son seemed strangely silent on Konrad's personal and private life. If the truth be known, the Mayor was a little intimidated by Konrad. Farr was right, Konrad was stealing his thunder. Konrad was getting above himself. In short, it was the Mayor's intention to re-establish his authority.

Konrad entered and they shook hands.

'Delighted you could spare the time. I know how busy you always are. Wine?'

Konrad noticed the Mayor's chain of office was hanging informally from the back of a chair. He accepted the offer of refreshment with a nod and a smile.

'So, how are you, my dear fellow?' asked Mr Flagg when they were settled in comfortable chairs and puffing on cigars. It was the Mayor's habit never to wait for an answer to his questions when nervous.

'Heard about that business with Skully. Dreadful man, ghastly, you certainly taught him a lesson, eh...'

Flagg forced out a strained chuckle. He flicked his cigar-ash into the fire, he felt hot.

Konrad seemed elsewhere.

'Some more wine?'

Flagg ladled in some more wine without waiting for an answer.

'I know what it's like after a hard day's - heard you like a drop too. Am I right? Nothing wrong with it, need time to unwind. I understand, nothing - no harm.'

Konrad, it seemed to him, was not there. He was looking now, like an effigy, through him. Flagg squirmed uncomfortably in the comfortable chair.

'Too hot for you?', he asked, moving his head from side to side to attract Konrad's attention.

'Can I open a window for you?'

Konrad's face remained immobile, placid.

'My son, Julius, tells me...actually my son doesn't tell me very much.' He attempted a collusive chuckle. 'Anyhow, bright lad, and very...are you sure it's not too hot for you? Yes, very impressed by your...you - by you....Anyhow, as I was saying...what was I saying?'

Flagg's discomfort mounted steadily. He tugged at his cravat and gulped from his glass.

'Oh yes, magnificent reports on the progress of the children. Everyone is very, all very - how is it that you manage to - discipline, I suppose? I'd be very interested to, I can tell - let me put it this way, I can sense a fellow believer in, what shall I call it? Discipline, I suppose.' He let out a high laugh, a gasping squeal of a laugh. 'I'm losing,' he thought to himself, 'I don't feel...'

'Rigid,' he continued, 'rigid, and rigidity, and -'

Flagg's mouth was open fully. He licked his lips and watched with fascination as Konrad took a folded paper bird from the inside pocket of his gown.

'Absolute necessity for rigidity and stability, don't you think? Eh?' continued Flagg, desperate now to shut up. '...for the whole Province I mean, not too harsh of course, I hope, not necessary to resort to the barbaric methods resorted to by Skully and his kind, his despicably filthy kind. Of course in my boyhood, Oh! my boyhood! How we used to suffer at the hands of our Schoolmaster. How rigid he was, how, unimaginable hells oh I can't tell you, my boyhood, terrible mistake we made in employing him - I made in, in the first place, scum if the truth be known, soon as he walked through the town gates - stinking, scum-sucking, arse-licking - should have sentenced him to be flogged, flayed alive, and be thanked for it - pain - I would have done it with my bare hands, I should have reached out and grabbed the bastard by the throat and throttled him with my bare hands until...'

Flagg started crying, the tears streaming down his purple face, 'until his eyes were dangling on his cheeks - the dirty, dirty, swinish, pig-swine beast! beast! beast! beast!...'

Flagg's eyes seemed to be extending out of their sockets as he watched Konrad throw the paper bird into the fire, and his smile disappear.

The Mayor's face turned from purple to pure grey. Throwing himself into the back of his chair, he recoiled from Konrad as though he had grasped a hot poker. With one hand he yanked at his cravat desperately, sending buttons flying across the room, and with the other grabbed wildly at his chest, twisting the flesh at his breast, ripping open his waistcoat and tearing the cloth of his shirt.

Konrad stood up, and helped himself to a generous glass of wine.

'Delicious wine, Mr Mayor. Since there seems to be a lull in the conversation may I take the opportunity to thank you for your support, but may I also add I am merely laying the foundation for a grand scheme, the aim of which I suspect you would not approve of.'

Stimulated by the excellent wine, Konrad elaborated on his future plans for the children of Aln.

'First, they are about to take control of the School budget. This is the way they will learn the practical use of mathematics and economic principles.

'Secondly, an argument between two or more pupils will occasionally occur. This is politics, and an opportunity for them to learn the principles of political and diplomatic negotiation, and its incipient pitfalls.

'Thirdly, I am about to implement a half-day. The children are far too seeking now to be contained in one place for an entire day. Time spent in study must be balanced with production and creation. We will spend the morning in study and discussion, the afternoon in the workshops and fields learning useful crafts and skills.

'Fourthly, I will brook interference from no one.

'Fifthly, your son will be my successor.

'Sixthly, abstract knowledge and ideology is the enemy of progress, of value. I have come to destroy it.

'As for you, your future does not look so promising. A raging pain crashes in your breast and head which is almost unbearable, but you will not die. You will not die for some time, and before you die you will lose all sense of joy and sorrow, you will feel nothing for anyone, not even yourself. You will be consumed by frustration, with the knowledge that you will have to go away without having made the slightest mark on history, that your life has been meaningless, that whatever you dreamed of doing it is now too late to achieve. You will remain alive long enough to see those dearest to you forget you, and long enough to see me seduce your beautiful young wife.'

After finishing the dregs of the wine, Konrad wiped his face and mouth carefully with a handkerchief. He bowed to the Mayor, who hardly seemed to notice. His eyes were glazed and his tongue was lolling uselessly from the side of his mouth.

Konrad opened the door and shouted, 'Please, someone help, assistance for the Mayor ! The Mayor is ill, help for the

Mayor !'

All passions begin with an exchange of glances.

There was no mistaking the glance that Konrad and Mrs Flagg gave one another.

Konrad took a full and penetrating look at her dark hair, delicate features, firm breasts and lithe body.

'If there is anything I can do...?' he asked her in the corridor afterwards.

'Please stay to dinner, Mr Konrad.'

Konrad bowed.

'If it will be of comfort to you, I will.'

The New Year Celebration and The Grand Donation were magnificent and an unqualified success. Konrad conducted the children in Holy Song in the Square on New Year's morning and they sang like angels.

'Monster,' Skully was heard to snarl. He was reduced to water-carrying since after his accident he was unable to hold a pen.

Officers accompanying the Agents who came to collect the Donation Box had brought with them a wide selection of souvenirs from New Jerusalem - pictures showing the magnificent buildings and gardens, grains of sand from outside the Temple itself, twigs, pebbles and leaves, and they were eagerly snapped up.

The Church was ablaze with candles during the Grand Donation. From the pulpit, adorned with holly and ivy, Mr Map said it had been a good year, and prayed to the Anointed One to shower good fortune down on the poor citizens of Aln. Gammy showed everyone his new pair of shoes that had appeared mysteriously outside his door that morning.

Mr Flagg spent the celebrations at home.

After a thorough examination of the shell that had once contained the Mayor, the Doctor declared he would never walk or speak again. He diagnosed complete physical and mental breakdown, the worst case he had ever encountered, brought on by the great strain of his responsibilities.

After the Donation, Konrad stood everyone who was crowded into the parlour of The Weavers' Arms a drink of whatever they pleased.

Celebrations continued long into the night.

'Off we go!' commanded Konrad.

It was quite a sight to see him, silk vermilion gown flapping in the wind, leading the children out of the Schoolhouse, across the old bridge and into the artisan quarter.

Never before during School hours had the townspeople seen children on the streets of Aln. And Konrad had arranged for them to observe and learn how to make candles, dipped and moulded. How thrilled the children were, how well-drilled, and how quickly they learnt.

As the weeks passed to Spring they were to learn all the secrets of their parents' trade. After they had mastered the art of candlemaking, and each child was able to make a perfect candle, wick central, with the correct mixture of fat and beeswax, they tackled stone-laying. Then potting, dyeing, locksmithing, weaving, carpentry, plastering, silversmithing, shoemaking, glazing, breadmaking. When the weather was warmer they left the town and explored the slopes. They learnt how to plant different seeds, trail vines, press olives, keep bees, and how to till and husband the soil.

They worked with a vigour and enthusiasm that surprised the artisans, that even shocked them.

Konrad encouraged the children to question everything they did not understand or agree with. Clea Farr proved adept at weaving cloth, so that within a month all the children were wearing clothes woven by her.

Walter Snell mastered the secrets of locksmithing and invented more and more complex locks that the master locksmith could not unlock.

Oliver Tobler was a perfectionist when it came to stone-laying.

There were some voices of dissent, however, notably from among the Burghers of the Council, and particularly Mr Farr. 'They're jealous of children,' Konrad said, but on the whole his new educational method was thoroughly approved of.

During this period Konrad was at his happiest. He was no longer a simple Schoolmaster, but a facilitator, a creator of challenges, a creator of value. His mission was to establish a clear purpose for seeking minds and offer unstintingly his advice and guidance. It was at this time too that Julius was making great progress. Konrad was stricter with Julius than his own father had ever been. If Konrad wanted something done Julius strained every muscle and spent every ounce of energy in his body to ensure it was done. His vagueness had evaporated. His gaze was clear and penetrating like that of his master. He no longer found the need for self-mortification. He took over the preparation of Konrad's meals, much to the annoyance of Kitty, cleaned his linen, annotated his teachings, and ran around Aln carrying his messages.

'Remember our motto,' shouted Konrad to the children.

'Many in body, one in mind,' they chanted in unison.

'Good. I will no longer tolerate individual concerns disrupting the unity of the whole.'

'Communication and concern for the happiness of the whole can transcend any dispute. If you cannot transcend the differences you can leave now.'

No one moved.

'We are all different. What makes us strong is that we overlook difference. Without unity the power to progress will not be forthcoming, we will grind to a halt. You must not, under any circumstances, be responsible for the weakening of that power.'

It was as though the children all came from one family, sharing the confidence of a shared secret, and that secret was Konrad.

'Remember, we cannot be defeated by an enemy, however large, but we can be laid low by a tiny parasite in our bowels.'

Hugo Bull, who had proved a talented book-binder, began binding Julius' transcriptions of Konrad's lessons and oral teachings. Already they ran into several volumes.

16

One night in The White Hart, a most curious event took place.

A stranger had come to Aln to purchase mulberry dye and had rented a room for the night. After settling himself in and purchasing a tankard of wine, he entered into conversation with the landlord. What the stranger told him was soon attracting the notice of everyone in the parlour and was to create a considerable stir throughout Aln.

Some weeks previously, the stranger said, he had had the occasion to visit The City on business. He had stayed with his cousin, who was a night-watchman at the City Hall. It was his cousin who told him that something of great import had happened, and that the Electi were absolutely furious over it, some irregularity concerning the Grand Donation.

'Wait a minute,' said the landlord, 'how could your cousin know what the Electi were talking about? A night-watchman.'

'He didn't know exactly what was being said, but he can tell a lot by reading signs. For example, though he can't see them enter the building, because they each have their own key and secret entrance, he knows what they like to eat. There was one who always left messages, saying he wanted artichokes and butter. He loved his artichokes and butter this one did because he never ate anything else. So my cousin, he sort of pieced them together, their personalities and so forth, and he knows when they are replaced. Like one day there was suddenly no orders for artichokes and butter. Anyway, he knew something was up because they had just had their weekly meeting and suddenly they're all in for an all-night session. Later that day my cousin fell into conversation with an Intermediary with whom he was on friendly terms and he told him what was going on.'

'And?' asked the landlord.

'Well, apparently, someone had not placed money in the donation box but - a red button, and an unsigned letter addressed to the Electi.'

The drinkers in The White Hart stared at the stranger in disbelief.

'Of course the Intermediary swore my cousin to secrecy, but us being family and all -'

'What did the letter say?' asked the landlord, almost not wanting to know.

'Well...' said the stranger, licking his lips, relishing the attention.

'My cousin didn't know.' There was a groan of disappointment.

'But what he did say was he could tell the letter had been passed down to the Lesser Electi, and when they read it there were groans and cries and there was a commotion throughout the City Hall, a definite air of what he termed, "Panic!"'

The stranger poured himself another tankard of wine, neglecting to leave any money on the bar.

'This is terrible,' said Billy Payne, who was one of the most pious present. 'It will bring bad fortune down on The City.'

'Who would do such a thing?' asked another.

'No one knows,' answered the stranger, 'but one thing's for certain - when they catch the culprit he'll be for it.'

'But how will they know who did it? The letter was unsigned,' said the landlord.

'Oh, they have ways,' the stranger continued mysteriously. 'They're not called the Electi for nothing.'

'If I could get my hands on the bastard,' said a heavy drinker, punching the air.

'The rumour is that they're going to send out investigators to each region and they won't stop until they've got their man.'

This information made the drinkers doubly agitated. They stared at the stranger suspiciously.

'And how do we know that you're not an investigator?' asked the landlord, voicing the others' immediate thought.

'Don't be daft,' retorted the stranger, annoyed at losing his status as one in the know.

'You might be testing us, looking for guilty faces.'

The circle around the stranger dispersed as quickly as it had formed.

'If I was an investigator I wouldn't be blabbing my mouth off, would I?'

Some of the most worried went home immediately.

'If I was you I'd leave Aln tonight,' advised the landlord, 'otherwise you might find yourself leaving with your guts in a bag.'

Within a day everyone in Aln had heard the news, but it was not discussed openly.

When Julius told Konrad he expected a strong reaction but instead he hardly registered a flicker of interest. He sat in his chair and thought. Julius waited patiently until Konrad finally said, 'There is one thing which no one seems to have realized.' He looked grave. 'How did the Electi know?'

Julius silently mouthed the question before asking, 'Know what?'

Konrad scowled.

'Julius, I'm surprised at you - how did the Electi know what was in the envelope?'

Julius shrugged.

'Aren't the Donation envelopes placed anonymously in padlocked iron boxes to which only the Minister of the Great Temple of New Jerusalem himself has the key? Aren't the boxes shipped to New Jerusalem under armed escort? Aren't the envelopes only opened in the Temple by the most trustworthy acolytes, a ceremony that is itself said to last three days...so how did the Electi know?'

Julius flushed. 'As soon as the outrage was discovered in New Jerusalem the Electi were informed?'

'By my calculation that would be impossible. By custom

64

the boxes are shipped on the fourth day of the first month. At the very least, provided the sea crossing was smooth and good time was made overland, the journey would take eight weeks. And what is the date today?'

Julius' face turned ashen as he understood Konrad's implication.

'The eighth of the fourth month,' he whispered.

'Also, it would take at least six weeks for a messenger to return from the Holy Land, would it not? It is therefore impossible that any message could have reached The City from New Jerusalem before the Electi met to discuss it.'

Julius slumped to the ground and held his head.

'I conclude therefore that the box or boxes must have been opened in The City before they were dispatched to New Jerusalem - if indeed they were!'

Julius' head was swirling, he felt as though he were about to vomit. He needed to think this through. The implications, the enormity of what Konrad was saying called so much into question that -

'All...' said Konrad with a flourish, 'is not as it is supposed to be.'

17

After the rumour caused by the stranger refused to die down, Mr Map, urged by the other members of the Council, reluctantly agreed to speak about the matter from the pulpit. He was most put out by the incident and intended to say so.

The time would soon come when a new Mayor would have to be elected; the members of the Council were keen for the matter to be forgotten before the election, especially Mr Farr.

On the fourteenth day of the second month, as many as could crowded into the Church, and those who could not gathered in the Square in the rain. Mr Map began by quoting extensively from the Holy Book.

'Rejoice ye with Jerusalem, and be glad with her,' he thundered, 'that ye may suck and be satisfied with the breasts of her consolations, and be delighted with the abundance of her glory.'

He reminded the townspeople that New Jerusalem was not the mere earthly City, the anointed Kingdom -

'...and he carried me away in the spirit to a great and high mountain, and showed me that great City, the Holy New Jerusalem, descending out of heaven...and her light was like unto a stone most precious, even like a jasper stone, clear as crystal...

'It is essential that our Holy City, which would not be manifest but for the efforts of the Electi, be maintained in all magnificence for the return of Isa, a City fit for a Messiah. Every man, woman and child can play their part. And the day will come when vines shall appear, having each ten thousand shoots, and on every shoot ten thousand twigs...and every grape will give five-and-twenty barrels of wine. Throughout that time the stars shall be brighter, the brightness of the sun shall increase, and the moon shall not wane. Honey in abundance shall drip from the rocks and fountains of milk and wine shall burst forth. The Anointed One will supply us all with abundant food and there will be no labour or suffering, and all shall spend their last years in New Jerusalem with Him, unaging, marrying and begetting however many times as the earth pours forth its fruits, and who -'

Mr Map's eyes searched his congregation, a sea of wide and hungry mouths.

'Who?'

His preparation had been thorough. He swayed back and forth.

'Who...does not want to live in such a place?'

Gammy put his hand up, but no one took any notice.

'Who would not spare a ri to build such a Kingdom? He who would not would be as simple as poor Gammy there.'

Mr Map then turned to the subject everyone had come to hear.

'Now, there has been some loose talk, originated by the hearsay of a stranger that the donation box was opened in The City before its despatch to the Holy City. That man, that...stranger, should have been cast off the town walls, and his body dashed to pieces on the rocks for spreading such a lie. And I want none of you - none of you to ever repeat such a lie again, let us pray.'

Everyone was most impressed with Mr Map's sermon. Rarely had they seen him so impassioned. But they were not totally convinced; doubts were still expressed in the taverns. Church attendance increased and the confession box was rarely empty. All strangers come to buy or sell at the Market were shunned for fear of their being Investigators. With Konrad's permission, and a promise not to be too long about it, Julius was one of those moved to confess. But in fact it was quite some time before he emerged from the booth, and when he did he was seen to be greatly agitated and to have tears in his eyes. Mr Map was also most put out, and staggered from the booth, making his way to the altar, where he prayed fervently.

As he was filing out of the Church after the sermon, Konrad felt a tug at his sleeve.

'Why is the moon more useful than the sun?' Gammy asked him.

'I don't know, Gammy, why is that so?' answered Konrad.

'Because at night we need more light.'

Konrad stared at Gammy's expectant face, long enough for curious onlookers to gather. He then took out his handkerchief and wiped away the flecks of spittle from Gammy's chin.

'Thank you, Gammy,' he said in a sincere and quiet voice. 'Thank you.'

Then, to the amazement of the onlookers, Konrad began to cry.

18

Konrad increased the speed and diversity of activities at the Schoolhouse to such an extent that some said it hardly resembled a School at all.

'More like a headquarters,' they said.

'He knows what he's doing,' said his defenders.

The children spent less and less time in the classroom and more and more in the artisan quarter. There were constant comings and goings, with each child receiving through instruction from Konrad privately. Julius supervised the schedules and continued with the task of amassing and editing Konrad's sayings and teachings.

'And you,' he told Julius, 'are living proof of my theories !'

As the spring progressed to summer, an additional room that the children were building in the inner courtyard was nearing completion. Oliver Tobler was delighted his technical design had made the transformation to stone without a single alteration. The new room, built at a fraction of the cost it would have taken had Mr Bock done it, was to house the enormous overspill of books that Konrad had accumulated. Practically every week a packet or box of books would arrive from The City, all for use by the children.

It was around that time also, before the party to celebrate the completion, that Julius hit a bad patch. He was constantly tired, irritable and sluggish. It had started after his confession to Mr Map. Konrad was very strict with him, never indulging his prize pupil, until finally seeing he had ground to a halt, he said, 'Now is the time you can make the greatest stride forward! At the darkest hour, when you feel hopeless, in a pit of despair, that is when the greatest possible value can be created. If you give in

69

now all your work will be lost.'

'Sir...' said Julius plaintively, 'I have reached my capacity.'

'Rubbish! Impossible! You are digging through the rubble of provisional ideas, your body aches, it's covered in bruises and cuts, that is what you feel. If you stop now, how can you find the gold that is another inch away from your fingertips?'

A tiny glint appeared in Julius' dull and bloodshot eyes.

'It takes sixteen days to walk to The City. If you stop on the fifteenth how can you expect to enjoy it's delights?'

Julius was smiling now. Konrad's encouragement never failed to rouse him. 'Never! - never have I heard of winter failing to turn into spring...have you?'

'No sir,' said Julius, his eyes sparkling with determination.

'Take a day off, eat, sleep, restore, but do not, do not give in to negligence.'

Konrad's reputation in Aln soared. There seemed no end to his knowledge or his patience. He knew how to cure stammers, how to teach patience to the frenetic and enliven the sluggish. The melancholic roared with laughter after a short time in his company.

Roger the Barber was famous for being the most miserable and tight-fisted man in Aln. One morning Konrad entered his shop and asked him, 'How much for a haircut?'

'Half a ri,' said Roger gruffly.

'How much is it for a shave?'

'Quarter ri.'

'Well shave my head then!'

Roger stared miserably at Konrad for a moment, then his shoulders began to twitch and heave.

'Shave my - ... Ha, ha, ha, ha, ha, shave my...'

His laughter drew a crowd outside the shop.

Julius had to start keeping an appointment book for those seeking guidance, though Konrad's solutions were always simple.

'I lent a man twenty ri,' whispered a locksmith in Konrad's ear, 'but there were no witnesses. Now I'm afraid he will deny having anything from me.'

Konrad answered immediately, without having to think at all.

'Invite him to your favourite tavern for a drink, and say in front of your friends, "I lent you forty ri," and he will shout, "What! You only lent me twenty," then you will have your witnesses.'

There was also respect for Konrad's compassion. Once he was passing a fat man sitting on a donkey that refused to move. The man beat the donkey about the ears with a stick. Konrad snatched the stick out of the fat man's hand and said, 'Stop beating this donkey! And give thanks that you are riding the donkey and it is not riding you.'

Such was the fat man's remorse that he dismounted, got down on his hands and knees and kissed the hooves of the donkey.

Of course, not everyone approved of Konrad's unconventional ways.

Skully was still nursing what most thought was an unreasonable grudge. He had taken to sniffing around the Schoolhouse after dark, peering through the windows to see...Once he had grabbed a child by the arm, to try and squeeze information out of him, but he was met with a firm but polite rebuff. Perhaps it was Skully who started the rumour that a servant looking through the keyhole into Mrs Flagg's bedroom had seen her opening her blouse and offering her breasts for Konrad to suck and squeeze them.

It was, however, most fortunate that Walter, who was employed at the Post Office, and a regular drinker at The Weavers' Arms, intercepted a letter that Skully had posted.

'First, Skully never normally sends letters at all,' Walter told Konrad. 'Secondly it was addressed to the Council of Electi.'

'Well done, Walter, well done. I would be most grateful to know who is posting letters to the Electi, or indeed, The City, perhaps, if you have time. Copies?'

'Only too pleased to be of help,' smiled Walter.

Three weeks later, Skully, whose job it was to carry a constant supply of water from the fountain to the artisans, lost his job for being drunk and unpunctual. It had been back-breaking work, but at least it had kept him in crusts. To make matters worse, he was replaced by the manure-carrier, a former beggar. It was too much for Skully. The next day he disappeared.

'Good riddance,' said one to another.

'He probably thinks he can make a new life for himself in The City.'

'Yes, perhaps he could find himself a job as a candle-snuffer,' and they both laughed.

19

On the third day of the sixth month, Mr Flagg the Elder, eighty-seventh Mayor of Aln, died in his sleep.

The Schoolhouse and all workshops were closed for a day of mourning. The corpse was laid out in an open coffin in the Church for the townspeople to pay their respects. It had been the intention of the Council to observe the custom of burial after the seventh day of death, but the rapid decay of the corpse forced them to bury it on the fourth day. Though no one openly stated it, it was believed that because the Mayor's skin had turned black, he was already burning in hell.

The day after Mr Flagg had been consigned to the vaults, Konrad visited the Council Chamber and requested an interview with Mr Farr who, until the election of the new Mayor, was designated acting Mayor.

After pleasantries had been exchanged, Konrad asked, 'Is it written in the constitution that a Mayor must be elected from among the Burghers?'

The directness of the question took Mr Farr aback. There was a palpable chill in the air.

'Well...not necessarily, though it usually is the case.'

'Is that a yes or a no?'

'Well, in theory...no.'

'So anyone resident in Aln may, in theory, put himself forward for election?'

'...Yes,' said Mr Farr, eventually, taking off his pince-nez and wiping them with great concentration.

'Why do you ask?' he asked quietly, feigning indifference.

'I wish to formally request that the Council put my name forward for election.'

After Mr Farr had calmly escorted Konrad to the door he shouted for the Clerk and called an emergency meeting.

For the rest of the day, the Clerk brought innumerable boxes from the basement archive and the Burghers examined the Town Constitution and every relevant document, for a reason why Konrad could not stand for election. They found that though the Mayor of Aln had not always been a member of the existing Council, he had always been a member of one of the five wealthiest families, descendants of the first men who settled on the hill.

'I can't understand it,' said Mr Snell, 'there's nothing here, why the hell didn't they make it law?'

'I always said this would happen one day,' said Mr Bock disgustedly.

'The only requirement is that the applicant be resident in Aln,' repeated Mr Farr distractedly.

'You're all worrying needlessly,' said Mr Map. 'Konrad is a powerful citizen, that is true, but he is not an Aln man by birth, and that's what counts. People would never accept him no matter how popular he is.'

'The people,' snorted Mr Farr, 'the people can't be trusted with making the right decision. The people can't be trusted to wipe their own bottoms properly and that's why we're here.'

'Farr's right,' said Mr Map, 'they love him. He's a born leader.'

'Map, with all due respect to your age and eminence - shut your mouth,' said Mr Farr. 'The election of Konrad would create a tremendous problem, a great upheaval. He's an odd man for all his brilliance and I don't trust him, how dare he come here and, he's a...'

'He's only a Schoolmaster,' said Mr Snell.

'He's a dangerous man who must be thwarted. I repeat, must.'

Mr Farr pored over the small hill of manuscripts on the Council table until late into the night. The next morning, the names of all the candidates were nailed to the huge studded Chamber door. The candidates were Mr Farr, Mr Map, Mr Snell, Mr Bock, Mr Bull, and Konrad.

For the next seven days the merits of each candidate were hotly debated in every tavern, workshop and home in Aln.

It was forbidden for any of the candidates to speak to anyone about the election, though privately, at night, visits were made by family members, and promises made. Konrad drank in The Weavers' Arms as usual, brushing aside any displays of support with a modest wave of his hand. As the days passed the arguments grew fierce, and fights became frequent.

Election day was fine and warm. Each Quarter had its allotted hour to cast its vote. When all the votes had been counted it was found that a tradition of Aln had been broken. With the exception of five votes, every cross was marked against the same name - Konrad's.

20

On the day of his first Council Session, the Mayor of Aln moved out of his rooms at The Weavers' Arms at dawn, and into the Council Chambers.

Kitty waved a tearful farewell and Konrad promised that his new appointment would not prevent him from dropping in for a glass now and then.

When the Burghers made their way silently across the Square they saw Konrad standing on the balcony of the Chamber with his arms outstretched.

'Welcome, Gentlemen!' he shouted across the Square, 'a new day begins.'

When they were all settled around the meeting table Konrad began.

'Mr Bull, I want a complete and detailed account of the moneys at the disposal of the Council as soon as possible.'

'As you wish,' said Mr Bull sullenly.

'Mr Snell, I will require a list of all cases to be tried, at your earliest convenience. I wish to acquaint myself with the workings of Aln and begin work immediately. Mr Map, may I please have a list of subjects and headings of all the sermons you intend giving until the end of the year?'

'Now look here -'

'I want to know everything. Mr Bock, please provide me with a list of all public works, with drawings and budget, that are at present to be undertaken.'

'But Mr Konrad,' retorted Mr Bock, 'it was the - I have never, it has never been deemed necessary in the past for me to account for my intentions, and I can assure you -'

'We are not living in the past, Mr Bock,' responded

Konrad. 'I have appointed Julius Flagg as my replacement at the Schoolhouse. I trust that meets with your approval ? I intend to devote my energies to my office.' Konrad turned to Mr Farr, whose head had been lowered since entering the Chamber. 'Mr Farr, please publish the following information. I want it known that in order for us to be of true service any citizen of Aln may visit me at the Council Chamber at any time, day or night, no matter how trivial the matter may seem. We don't want to give the impression to our townspeople that decisions regarding their lives are being made in secret, do we?'

Mr Farr smiled condescendingly.

'If I might suggest, Mr Mayor, such an arrangement would be extremely inconvenient. We are after all primarily a fiscal and administrative body. Our duty is to run an efficient and ordered town.'

'Mr Farr, I want the private made public not the public made private. Gentlemen, Aln is a town rich in treasure, of the body, that is skills. It is comparatively rich in treasures of the storehouse. What it is not abundant in is the treasures of the heart. And it is the accumulation of treasures of the heart that I intend to encourage. Do you agree?'

The Burghers were stubbornly silent. Konrad sprang up from his chair and paced the window overlooking the Square.

'Gentlemen, you are frightened of change. You are frightened of losing face, frightened of being alone, frightened of death, frightened of life. But as the Greek Heraclitus so rightly pointed out, "All is change."'

He returned to the room and began pacing the length of the table.

'It is my wish that not a single one of us will lie on our deathbed and feel remorse, or even the slightest regret. We shall all realize our full potential and experience the greatest happiness possible for a human being. We shall be an example for every town in the Province, indeed - The City itself!'

Mr Farr's head rose; all heads followed Konrad's pacing.

'Is that not an aim worth fighting for, Gentlemen? To die

for your town, to die knowing you have made your mark on its history, that it has become a better place through your efforts?'

Konrad's eyes blazed, his resonant voice pierced their hearts. After some moments of silence, Mr Map began to clap hesitantly.

'Here, here,' murmured Mr Farr sheepishly.

Konrad's blue eyes scanned the other Burghers. They too began to clap, gently at first, then louder and enthusiastically, Konrad joining in and increasing their pace. Then they cheered and sprang to their feet with tears in their eyes.

Konrad quietened them gradually by waving his arms.

'Gentlemen, to show our appreciation and respect to the townspeople we have the honour to serve, I propose we host a Grand Dinner to celebrate my inauguration.'

'That is the custom, Mr Mayor, preparations are already under way,' gasped Mr Map.

'You misunderstand me, I don't mean a small gathering of dignitaries in the Council Chamber, I mean a great feast for every inhabitant of the Town, to be held in the Square!'

'That's an absolutely fantastic idea,' said Mr Farr, wringing his hands with excitement.

'And as a show of goodwill, I suggest that you organize the dinner and serve the people with your own hands.'

'You mean cook?' asked Mr Bull querulously, 'I've never - I don't think I could -'

'You will need help, of course, but it will be your task to ensure the Dinner is a great success. You will hire the most expert cooks in Aln, and pay them well. And you will be, well...waiters!'

'Seconded,' said Mr Bock.

'Carried,' said Mr Farr triumphantly.

That night, Konrad pored over the Town Constitution, making copious notes in its margin.

When its blood was sufficiently warmed, the wall-lizard slithered out of a cleft in the limestone rock at the foot of the southern wall and darted through the olive trees. Though wall-lizards were common around Aln, they were so cleverly disguised they could only be noticed when they moved. Their bodies were covered in lines and spots which merged with their surroundings. They could disappear before your very eyes.

The lizard scuttled over the sandy soil, following its most favourite smell, the smell of ants. Its sensitive nose led it to a massive swarming of ants and though it was unsure about climbing and clinging to the sticky surface on which they were swarming, such an opportunity was too good to miss.

The lizard gorged itself until it could not eat one more ant. Swinging its bloated body through a mass of sticky, curly hair, it leapt back to the soil to find some shade. It was so bloated that it reluctantly had to ignore a solid mass of ants further on, burrowing through the palm of the hand.

By the time they discovered Skully's body, it could only be identified by the clothes.

An unfortunate suicide was the verdict of Mr Snell, the Serjeant-at-Arms.

When details of the Grand Dinner were nailed to the Council Chamber door they caused great excitement. Mr Bock commissioned a carpenter to construct a table long enough to encircle the whole Square.

Mr Snell was responsible for the wine and spirits, Mr Farr for composing the menu, and Mr Map for crockery and utensils and readying the cavernous Council kitchen.

'We'll have to send out for more, there's not near enough,' said Mr Map anxiously.

'Take whatever actions you think necessary in order to achieve your goal,' Konrad told him.

'Yes, Mr Mayor,' said Mr Map, bowing deeply.

It was many years since the great ovens in the Council Chamber had been lit. All the cauldrons and grid-irons were caked with rust and filth, but Mr Map set about his task with great alacrity.

Mr Bull was responsible for budget and accounts.

The Council Chambers had never been so busy. All day long there were frantic discussions and arguments, comings and goings, deliveries and despair, as the Burghers grappled with their jobs. And overseeing all was Konrad, sometimes chiding, sometimes sympathetic, always prepared to listen and always masterful. It was not his intention to solve their problems.

Mr Map came to him in despair one morning.

'Please try harder,' Konrad told the tearful old man. The kitchen seemed dirtier and more chaotic when Konrad inspected it than when the cleaning operation began.

'I want every pot and fork gleaming like the first day they were minted,' said Konrad comfortingly, wrapping a strong arm around Mr Map's shrunken shoulders.

'If I hadn't thought you were capable of accomplishing the task I wouldn't have asked you, would I? You will experience deep satisfaction when it is done, I promise.'

'Thank you, Mr Mayor,' said Mr Map, slightly happier.

At the end of each evening, Konrad held a meeting in the Council Chamber where each Burgher gave a progress report.

On the third night before the Grand Dinner, he called them to order.

'Thank you, Gentlemen - Mr Bock?'

Mr Bock rose to his feet immediately.

'I'm pleased to report that the tables and benches are finished and installation will begin at dawn tomorrow. The initial problem of the unevenness caused by the cobbles will be remedied by bedding down each bench in a layer of straw and earth.' Mr Bock lowered his eyes shyly. 'My own idea, if I may say so.'

'Well done, Mr Bock,' said Konrad.

He sat down to a round of applause, which made him blush.

Next was Mr Snell.

'The wine, enough for an army, is at this very moment stored in the cellar below us. There are four sorts of hock, claret, vintage and ordinary, rum eggnog, spiced posit, and beer, malt, and grain and cider.'

There was another tremendous round of applause, and then it was Mr Bull's turn.

'Though there are one or two further expenditures that I anticipate, as well as some unforeseen, for which I am also prepared, we are still well within our original budget; indeed, we have spent a third less than I calculated, due to the careful economies, and the goodwill of the townspeople.'

This drew a loud cheer and slaps on the table.

Next was Mr Farr. 'There is still some work to be done, balancing and so forth, and to ensure - at the insistence of our beloved Mayor - it is a healthy one, but in the main the menu is complete. We have topside beef, sirloin, brisket, fillet; we have chicken, pork and trout, seasoned with sorrel, dill, bay and fennel, served with mushrooms, haricots, runner and scarlet beans, parsnips, onions, garlic, pumpkin, avocado, followed by a choice of whortleberry, gooseberry or billberry pie, with cream.'

Groans of delight greeted Mr Farr's menu, giggles and jokes. Then the laughter died when they realized who was next to speak.

'Mr Map,' said Konrad. Mr Map had found his tasks particularly difficult, perhaps through debility and old age, several times he had threatened to give up.

He wrung his red and chapped hands and stood up wearily.

'The kitchen awaits your inspection, Mr Mayor, but it is, I believe, the cleanest and most well-appointed, efficient kitchen in the Province.'

This announcement elicited the loudest cheer of all and brought tears to Mr Map's eyes. Konrad called for wine and when it arrived and each had a glass in his hand, Konrad declared, 'Gentlemen, my confidence in you has been proved. Our success is assured.'

Mr Farr offered a toast too.

'The Mayor of Aln,' chorused the Burghers.

Mr Bock then tapped his glass hesitantly.

'We have taken the liberty of building a dais for you to preside over the Grand Dinner, and we would be most honoured if you would sit at the head of the table as it were.'

'You should have consulted me first,' said Konrad sternly.

'We paid for it out of our own pocket,' blurted out Mr Bull.

'In that case,' said Konrad, breaking out into a grin, 'I accept, but only that I may be in full view of the townspeople.'

23

The night before the Grand Dinner, none of the Burghers slept a wink.

In the hour before dawn they were all up, dressed and hurrying through the streets to the Chamber, for a final briefing from Konrad.

He was sitting in his private rooms, relaxed and cheerful in a brightly coloured dressing-gown. They clustered around him and his smile gave them confidence in spite of themselves.

'Now remember,' he said, pouring them each a strong small coffee, 'we are here to serve. We are to be polite at all times, courteous and humble. We are to anticipate difficulties and smooth away incidents. We are the ones who take responsibility for all...understood?'

'But -' began Mr Farr, but Konrad stopped him with a glance.

'Never say but, say and - any questions...then to your posts.'

The Burghers bowed. Konrad began his ablutions.

All through the day Konrad casually wandered through the sites of activity, smiling and humming to himself, chatting with the excited townspeople. He descended the narrow stone staircase to the vast smoke-filled kitchen, where huge ovens were belching and crackling heat, and great cauldrons and spits were turning in the enormous fireplaces.

The Square was magnificent. The table encircled the walls and huge, brightly coloured banners hung from the buildings. By late afternoon every space on the benches was taken by the townspeople who came in all their finery, and the anticipation was palpable.

At six o'clock there was a hush. The sky was a deep blue as the sun was dipping behind the mountains, giving the Council Chambers a bright orange glow. Suddenly, Konrad emerged on the balcony and strode along the ramp to his table and chair on the dais.

'I've never seen him look so well,' said one woman.

'I've never really thought him handsome before,' said her friend.

'Please accept my little supper as a token of my gratitude for appointing me your Mayor,' Konrad's voice echoed through the Square.

A roar of approval rippled through the assembled crowd.

Konrad picked up his glass.

'To Aln!'

'To Aln!' replied all present, with one voice.

During the meal Konrad wandered the whole length of the Square, shaking hands, chatting and joking. The townspeople could hardly believe the trouble the Council had gone to; the quality of the cooking was far beyond what most of them were used to. No one felt they were able to fully express their gratitude to Konrad.

When the meal was over the drinking continued late into the night.

One after another plucked up the courage to stagger to the dais to ask Konrad for some favour or other. Some who had admittedly been unable to resist satiating themselves, were not too coherent; one or two even retched up in full view of the Mayor. But Konrad received them all with good grace and extended his invitation to them all to visit him whenever they wished.

As soon as the last person had left the Square, the clean-up operation, supervised by Mr Bock, went into full swing, the Burghers almost drunk with tiredness, and it continued until dawn. Every gush, dribble and crumb was cleaned away, and when the inhabitants of Aln eventually emerged from their beds, blinking in the sun, it was as though the Grand Dinner had been a magnificent dream.

24

Konrad locked himself in his rooms for three days, telling the Burghers not to worry. On the fourth day, they were waiting in a line outside for his emergence. At nine o'clock precisely, Konrad came out. He was pale, but bristling with energy. Brushing past the Burghers, refusing the bread and milk posit, he strode down the corridors with the Burghers in tow to the Council Chamber.

'Gentlemen, as you know, I do not intend to merely carry things along as my predecessors have done, but totally transform this town, for the better naturally. Our first task, I have decided, will be to eliminate some problems. There are far too many cases of theft in Aln. I intend to stop it. I must ask for your total co-operation.'

The Burghers nodded dutifully, unable to comprehend. Then Mr Bull said, 'But that is impossible.'

'Is it? You say so, I say it is not.'

'It's human nature,' said Mr Map.

'I must insist you support any measure I propose. I propose to eliminate theft within one month.'

The Burghers shuffled uncomfortably.

'Will you support this campaign?'

Konrad's strength of purpose sent a thrill of anticipation through them.

They all agreed.

'Good. Now, why do people steal? It is because of the mistaken notion that happiness lies in acquiring material possessions. Stealing therefore is not the result of human nature but of an incorrect philosophy. I propose that all material possessions be held communally, including money, bedding, clothing, weapons, food, jewellry. Anything else that can be held and coveted will be placed in a central store, and may be drawn on by those who need it. In one fell swoop we will eliminate greed, poverty and theft. I guarantee it!'

'No one would agree to it,' said Mr Bull, the wealthiest man in Aln.

'Oh yes they will,' said Konrad.

'But how could such a measure be administered?' asked Mr Farr.

'I will take charge. Any citizen may ask me and I will decide whether their request is reasonable, whether they are truly in need of the goods they ask for. But private ownership of money will be abolished. Money will only be used when dealing with the outside. All work will be paid for in kind and receipts issued. Mr Farr, please call a public meeting for noon tomorrow in the Square. Mr Snell, see to it that every citizen attends.'

At noon precisely, Konrad stepped out onto the balcony of the Council Chamber to a loud cheer of approval which continued for some time. Motioning for silence, he addressed the crowd in a powerful voice.

'Citizens of Aln, why are we here?'

'Because we were born here!' shouted a young lad, to hoots of derision and laughter.

Konrad nodded. 'But why not move to The City?'

'Because we like it here,' answered another.

'Precisely, my friend. We like it here, because we feel safe, but I have a very important question for you now - what are we trying to achieve?'

A dead silence came over the crowd.

'What is the sum total of our lives today? Have we made profit? Will we all die in vain?'

How proud they were of their Mayor. Mr Flagg had never addressed them like this. Konrad was a man of the people.

'Many of us, I'm sure, have secret fears of the future. Others have secret dreams locked in their hearts that they are afraid to reveal, even to themselves. And why? Because you think you do not deserve to be happy. But how tragic it would be if, having been born into this magnificent Province, none of you fully realize these dreams. Do you want to die unfulfilled? Do you want to die with regret, thinking, "I never achieved what I wanted to because I was a coward"?'

'No,' someone shouted, echoed by many others.

'Then we must return to the world of childhood and regain the purity of freedom we had then, when our hearts were filled with indomitable hope, when everything was possible, when concern for others was as natural as for ourselves. We must all be like parents to one another, all display the unconditional love of a mother, extended to all. After all, there is only one Aln in the Province and it is yours -'

'And there is only one Mayor,' shouted someone jokingly but with sincerity.

'And I am yours,' rejoined Konrad.

Most of the assembled crowd had tears in their eyes, some crying openly, some cheering fiercely.

'Before I die, I have determined to ensure that every single one of you will become indescribably happy, and I will not stop until I have accomplished this. I ask for help from no one, because this task is the purpose of my entry into the world. I promise you...I will not fail!'

Some of those close to Konrad fainted, many fell to their knees in prayer, women groaned, and some were seized with convulsions.

'Private ownership will be abolished. Self-seeking is an abomination, buying and selling is an abomination, working for money is an abomination, usury is an abomination...And as the Holy Book says, "And the multitude of them that believed were of one heart and of one soul, but they had all things in common, neither was there any among them that lacked, for as many as were possessors of lands and houses sold them, and brought the prices of things that were sold, and laid them at the apostles' feet, and distribution was made unto every man according to his needs". Who among us citizens has the right to grow fat from the labour of his fellow creatures? It is the Anointed One's wish that we sacrifice our possessions and he will not be pleased until we do. He is angered by greed. He weeps bitter tears and his heart breaks to see his children so corrupt, and my friends - we must protect our children, we must guard them from the stinking putrefaction of our greed. Until such time as Aln is purged and pure they must stay with me in the Council Chambers, where they will no longer be befouled. Give up your children and save them! Give them up to me! And I will return them when the time has come!'

The edicts were passed by the deafening roar of the townspeople. Spontaneous singing broke out as they rushed to their homes to gather their possessions, and the Burghers' fingers ached with cataloguing the possessions and counting the money, which took three weeks.

25

Konrad's capacity for work was enormous, his hunger for change voracious. Whereas responsibility increased his energies and stature, the status and self-confidence of the Burghers decreased. They constantly sought his views and seemed unable to make even the smallest decisions without his approval. Women sought his advice on suitable marriage suitors or urged him to name their new-born babies. Disputes, however small, were brought before him and his word was final. Every second of his time was put to good use, he even gave advice while bathing, and the only time spent alone were the brief hours he snatched to sleep. Despite this gruelling schedule he never seemed to tire or begrudge anyone, indeed he was thriving. There was no doubt he was a man out of the ordinary, great things were expected, perhaps even a miracle. There were no more thefts but there were dissenters, particularly from among the formally wealthy five families.

'I expect you,' Konrad told the Burghers, 'to make every effort to win them over. And they must hand over the ri I know they have hidden, to avoid future unpleasantness.' He told Snell to double his Sarjeants.

One night there was a disturbance in The White Hart when a butcher had said that if anyone went against Konrad they would be arrested and bound to the posts of the Council Chambers. The Landlord told him to leave and drink elsewhere, and when he refused and continued to berate Konrad, he was taken outside and badly beaten.

And then, when the news of the edict reached the neighbouring towns in the region, beggars began to arrive, expecting to receive money simply by asking for it. Many of them slept along the balcony of the Council Chamber waiting for Konrad to appear. Konrad was lenient to them and sanctioned food to be distributed. But when they discovered they would not be given any money they spat in disgust on the Council door and left. And then there were the religious fanatics and lone penitents. They came to pledge their allegiance to the Mayor of Aln, and begged him to instruct them in spiritual discipline. These men Konrad dismissed contemptuously.

Julius returned from his round of the children's dormitories. All were asleep. By now the children did everything together, as though an inexorable rhythm pulsed through them. They were many in body with one shared mind. Even when they were apart, and one of them decided to do something, all the others determined to do the same.

Though it was late, Julius decided to catch up on some reading. The events of the last few weeks had left little time for pleasure.

His room was isolated, at the top of the Council Chamber overlooking the Square. Contained in it was a narrow bed, a table and chair, a wardrobe and a reading lamp. He lit the lamp and took out a book from his satchel. Sitting at the table he opened the book at its first page.

Halfway down the page Julius became aware of a buzzing somewhere in the room. He decided to ignore it and continue reading. After some moments, however, he found he could not ignore the buzzing and grew annoyed. Then a fly landed on the table in front of him. He peered over the top of the book to get a look at it. The fly was rubbing its forelegs against its head. This casual attitude annoyed him still further. Everything in the room was clean and tidy, he cleaned it every morning, and here was this stinking fly making itself at home.

Julius felt hot, and prickly. His anger was rising, he did not want this fly in his room. He closed the book gently and steadied himself to bring it crashing down on the fly. 'It'll be an honour,' he thought, 'for a fly to be killed by a book.' He slammed the book down decisively on the table. He smiled. Crouching down, making sure that the fly would not require further pressure to be exerted on it, he peeled away the book. There was no stain on the cover of the book. There was no fly. Then, he heard a voice say, 'What did you do that for? I love you.'

Julius froze for a moment. He looked round the room, there was no sign of the fly. He shrugged his shoulders, and settled down to resume reading his book. But his mood was soured, he was sorry not to have killed the fly.

Then the voice said, 'I want to be your friend...I am beautiful, am I not?'

Julius tried to ignore the fly, but he couldn't concentrate; the words of the page seemed not to be in the correct order. Suddenly, he felt something attach itself to his lower lip. His instinctive reaction was to wipe it off with the back of his hand. The fly clung on with its sticky pads. He brushed it again, more carefully this time, then felt a sting. That was it, he'd had enough, he started swearing violently; the pain was unbearable for such a small creature to have caused. And the buzzing was worse than ever. He spotted another fly, on the windowpane. He went over to the bed to pick up a pillow - he couldn't throw a book against the windowpane. He picked up the pillow, and released a black fog of angry flies...

26

First one person pointed at him, then others, hearing his shrieks, rushed to look out of their windows. Julius Flagg was running stark naked through the cobbled streets of Aln. When he ran into the Square a large crowd was following him, and saw him collapse and writhe spasmodically outside the Council Chamber.

When the frenzy was over, and he was no longer speaking in a strange language, which some thought was Hebrew, he froze in ecstasy.

'Should we move him?' asked someone.

'Not while he's communicating with Isa,' another insisted, 'He could die.'

The inhabitants of Aln, with a reputation for superstition, believed such frenzy to be the result of extreme sensitivity to the Anointed One. They stood around waiting to receive a message from heaven or witness the poor devil die in pain.

When Julius finally opened his eyes, scrambled to his feet in a daze and regained his bearings, he announced in a calm and sensible voice, 'The Anointed One has revealed to me the truth - Konrad is his prophet.'

Many palms were shown to the sky and there were shouts of 'Holy! Holy! Holy!'

'Woe is he who goes against the word of a prophet. He shall be called an unbeliever. The Anointed One has sent us Konrad to instruct us in preparation for his Kingdom upon earth!'

Women tore their clothes and spun round in circles. Some threw themselves on the ground and spread out their arms in the shape of a cross and ground their teeth. Some stood motionless, staring up at the sky.

'Konrad is his prophet and he has the ear of heaven. It has been decided that we shall experience the delights of paradise. Here we shall live according to Holy Law and not the laws of Man. It is Isa's will that we regain our innocence from before the Fall and be as naked and unashamed as Adam and Eve. We are the chosen ones! O Holy! Holy! Holy! is our town. O bless our state of innocence and save us in the last days!'

With this, Julius ran to the Council Chamber door and banged on it until it was opened and he was let in.

Konrad, who had been watching the incident from an upper window was very pleased.

Mr Snell sent out his men to disperse the crowds.

'Mr Chapman, sir, may I come in?' Kitty enquired.

'Enter,' answered a voice with the strong and unmistakable accent of The City.

'There's a note from the Mayor for you,' she said, handing him an unsealed envelope.

'Oh, really, and how is it you are able to tell?'

'Because I read it, how else do you think I know?' sneered Kitty.

Chapman was looking forward to leaving Aln as quickly as his work could be completed. He did not feel safe and was surprised at the speed with which the Mayor had sought him out.

> Dear Mr Chapman, I should be delighted if you
> would join me this evening at the Council Chamber,
> shall we say around nine? It is our custom to extend
> hospitality to all visitors to Aln. I am also always
> anxious to catch up with the latest news of The City.
>   Konrad.

Although Konrad had requested a list of all strangers left in

Aln after the close of the town gates to be handed in daily, Mr Chapman was the first to be invited to his private chambers.

At nine o'clock precisely, Mr Chapman was knocking on the iron-studded door and glancing around nervously. Strangely, no one had seemed to notice him as he had been escorted through the streets, as though they knew his purpose in visiting the town, but that was impossible. The image of a sacrificial lamb being led to slaughter had flashed through his mind.

A pair of eyes appeared at the grille and he was admitted at once. He followed a clerk along a narrow corridor, up a winding staircase and was shown into Konrad's private dining-room. He saw no one else along the way.

'The Mayor will be with you shortly,' said the Clerk, backing out of the room. Chapman was rather pleased to be left alone in what he took to be Konrad's private apartments. He glanced around quickly at the well-appointed room ablaze with candles, with well-trained eyes. There was nothing untoward he had to report. An illuminated manuscript of the *Teachings of Isa* lay open at a lectern, a long oak table was set for a feast and in the hearth resinous logs crackled and roared, filling the room with a sweet heavy smell.

Chapman thought he heard the sound of a child's laughter, resonantly amplified by the chimney, and put his head up it to make sure.

Even with his head up the chimney, Chapman could feel a presence. Freeing his head, he swung around to see Konrad smiling at him with his arms crossed.

'Welcome to Aln, Mr Chapman,' said Konrad, extending a hand, which against a previous decision, Chapman shook vigorously. Konrad possessed, as he had been briefed, a devastatingly charming smile, and a confidential manner that made you feel instantly welcome, indeed, that you were a most important person. Konrad made Chapman rise in his own estimation, and he found himself thanking Konrad profusely for his hospitality.

'Most kind of you, most considerate.'

As soon as they were seated and served an excellent onion and fennel soup, Konrad began to question his guest in a seemingly natural manner. Chapman had to remind himself of his mission and who he was talking to.

'What brings you to Aln, Mr Chapman, if you don't mind my asking?'

'No, not at all.' He had to be careful. He had intended to be cool, reserved and professional, trying to put Konrad on the spot at the start, but he found himself irresistibly attracted to Konrad. He knew very well from his training that the first few minutes of a meeting determined the whole, but he found that, rather than controlling the pressure, he was anxious to make a good impression on Konrad.

'I'm looking for a house to buy for my retirement, somewhere remote and...calm.'

'Ah. So that would explain your walking the streets throughout the day?'

'Indeed, I'm quite worn out by it, though Aln is such a beautiful town, so unspoilt, the City dwellers really have no idea, do they, if only they would take the trouble -'

'The grass is always greener, Mr Chapman, is it not?'

Chapman laughed warmly, genuinely. He intended not to laugh, but he was enjoying himself, the wines were excellent, and he felt an overpowering sense of well-being.

'And what news from The City?' asked Konrad, carving a leg of lamb.

'Oh, nothing changes, the usual worries, expenditure too high, endless tinkering and pontificating over the Code of Ethics.'

'And what line of work are you in exactly, if I may ask?'

'My job?' It was getting increasingly difficult. Chapman reminded himself again of his mission; he rubbed the back of his neck. He had not even expected to meet Konrad in person and here he was dining with him, and enjoying himself too. 'I'm a Senior Clerk, a mere pen-scraper.'

He had intended to make a few discreet enquiries - Konrad's background, origins - stay a few days to observe the populace and leave quietly, unnoticed. Despite his being the subject of an investigation, he liked Konrad, he liked Konrad a lot.

'A Clerk's wages must have risen considerably since I was last in The City, if you are thinking of buying another home,' said Konrad amiably. 'Perhaps you're prone to giving large sums of money to the Grand Donation to have such good fortune?'

At the words 'Grand Donation', Chapman's face flushed, in spite of his rigorous training.

'Yes, indeed, I try my best, you know, as I'm sure we all do, Mr Mayor.' He had to stop Konrad going along that line, and pull things back in his direction.

'Yes, nasty business about the - how shall I put it, perhaps treachery might not be too strong a word, the disrespectful taunting of the Electi themselves.'

'You are referring to the envelope that was tampered with?' said Konrad.

'Quite,' said Chapman, '- tampered with? I would hardly have said "tampered with".'

He leaned back in his chair in an attempt to relax.

'What did the note say?' asked Konrad.

'What did the - Oh Mr Mayor, you tease me, you know that the content of that letter was never disclosed by the Electi.'

'Not to the general public, no, I just thought that a man like yourself might know people in high places, have friends perhaps who might be personally acquainted with members of the Lesser Electi?'

'Oh stop teasing me, Mr Mayor,' said Chapman, rubbing the back of his neck ever more vigorously, 'as I say, I'm a mere pen-scraper.'

'You are too modest, I fear, Mr Chapman. After all, it is well-known that if there is a vacuum somewhere - the Electi will seek to fill it.'

'Vacuum?' Chapman cursed himself for being liberal with the fine wines.

'Is not that common parlance amongst Agents and

Intermediaries for a loss of influence in any part of the Province?'

Mr Chapman attempted a smile, shrugged his shoulders and grabbed at his wine-glass.

'Tell me, Mr Chapman, if a person who at some stage had met an incumbent member of the Electi, do you think they would recognize them as such instantly?'

'Of course.'

'By using signs?'

'Perhaps, one can only imagine. Mostly through signs, or perhaps just with their highly developed intuition.'

'So by using certain signs or phrases, a person who used them might be mistaken, by one who could read them, as a member of the Electi even though in actual fact he was not?'

'My dear Mr Mayor, I really have no idea.'

'No, I'm sure not. It is interesting to speculate nevertheless.'

Konrad rose to his feet and moved to the fireplace to warm his hands.

'I know one does not put oneself forward for election to the Electi. It is not even a question of wanting to be one. You simply are one, or become one in the same way as a caterpillar becomes a butterfly. You don't fill in a form. There is no form, choice is a result of actual human behaviour not so-called qualifications. You are chosen in a sense, but chosen by an evolutionary need.'

'Evolutionary need?'

'I'm only speculating, of course, but have you considered that rather than passing a test or something primitive like that, people chosen to act as Agents, or spies, for that is their function, by the Electi are chosen not for their strong beliefs but for their enormous capacity to serve?'

'Yes, and what happens to the Electi when they are no longer incumbent? Where do they go? Perhaps they undertake some kind of teaching mission that they discharge in mysterious ways, or are sent to live and work in New Jerusalem as a reward for services rendered.'

'Mr Mayor, I really think we ought to discontinue this conversation. It is not appropriate for such people as us, in positions of responsibility to - with all due respect - speculate on the subtle workings and intentions of the Electi. They communicate in ways we cannot possibly understand.'

'Oh, Mr Chapman, I am quite aware that it suits the Electi's purpose for the citizens of the Province not to know who their real leaders are.'

'What is the point,' said Mr Chapman, his anger rising, 'of being known to the public, to bask in recognition? Only the common person seeks to be recognized for their good works.'

'I can assure you, Mr Chapman, I have no desire to perpetuate memory of me in this world.'

'You, Sir?'

Konrad lost his smile, his eyes narrowed. Chapman tried to return his stare but he could not.

'I have nothing to hide, Mr Chapman, and that is my strength,' said Konrad. 'Anyone is free to visit Aln provided he does not try to change one iota, or think he has the right to instruct the Prophet.'

'I should think not,' said Chapman, eyes fixed on his glazed pears.

'Because there is something I would like all strangers to this town to realize and that is there is no vacuum in Aln. There is no sin, in the common parlance. And if The City should send out one of its Agents to search for sin he will not find one tiny miserable sin because Isa is in me and speaks with my tongue and Isa does not lie or sin. Just like Isa, I am eternal. I am born in time, born of the Anointed One, for all that the Anointed One has I have too. Isa was, in a sense, my predecessor. He lived and died for me, and he shall come to Aln to serve me once again...I think that is clear, Mr Chapman?'

'If you say so,' whispered Chapman, his eyes still glued to the pears.

'What I was I wished to be, and what I wished to be I already was. It is by my own free will that I have emerged. If I wished, I need not have become flesh and blood and I would not now be a creature. For the Anointed One can know, wish, be or do nothing without me. Like Isa I have created myself, I have created all things with him, and it is my hand that supports heaven and earth and all the other creatures - without me, nothing exists!'

'Holy! Holy! Holy! is the father,' cried Mr Chapman, shaking uncontrollably and stamping his feet furiously.

'Holy indeed, Mr Chapman, please pass one more detail to your influential friends in The City. Once liberated from sin, and re-integrated with the primal state of innocence enjoyed by Adam and Eve - we become sinless, incapable of sin, and therefore the Anointed One can to all intents and purposes be dismissed.'

'Holy! Holy! Holy!' chanted Mr Chapman continuously, until he slipped into unconsciousness...

27

During the tenth month, the number of visions seen, especially among women, increased substantially. They were invariably accompanied by screaming and writhing and dancing and exhibitions of nakedness. Something wondrous was about to happen.

Konrad passed another two Edicts.

One raised a levy of men to begin work on ramparts to be built at the base of the hill.

The second allowed Konrad to appoint and arm a personal guard of twenty men.

In the eleventh month, the Edict of Purification, as it came to be known, was passed unanimously.

All those who wished it could leave Aln and join the 'certain to be destroyed,' outside the gates, though Konrad had difficulty getting the Burghers to agree.

'It will turn the outside world against us,' argued Mr Farr.

'Then let them be against us,' said Konrad defiantly, 'We'll be ready for them when the time comes.'

Those people who decided to leave were derided, spat at and pelted with filth, which annoyed Konrad. It was bitter cold on the appointed day and raining, and it was a sorry sight to see them, old people mostly clutching babies, leaving behind all their belongings but for the clothes on their backs. They were to be forced to beg for food and shelter in the surrounding countryside until the Agents were sent from The City with money and to make arrangements for their rehabilitation. Only one person had received a message from Konrad asking them to stay and that was Kitty.

Now the town was inhabited solely by those Konrad

named 'the children of innocence,' in the first town in the Province without sin.

Towards the end of the twelfth month, Konrad made an inspection of the earthworks, in the company of their architect, Mr Bock. He was seen to be very pleased, but urged the workers to complete the work by the first day of the New Year.

Then came the Edict of Openness, which forbade anyone to lock their doors during the day or night.

'Anyone can enter where they wish,' announced Mr Farr from the balcony of the Council Chamber. 'Since everywhere belongs to everyone the difference between public and private is abolished.' There was a disturbance over this Edict that lasted for several days. It was the first Edict that Konrad had to enforce; he had to call a public meeting and spoke at some length.

'What are you afraid of? Why are you hiding from your fellow-citizens? What gives anyone the right to believe they deserve privacy?'

Privacy was declared sinful.

By the twelfth month, Konrad had appointed Officers, regular Night Watches and a fire service. The earthworks and the spiked trenches were on schedule for completion.

Lumb the Butcher confessed to Mr Bull that he had buried some gold coins and knew others who had done likewise. Konrad ordered his Officers to enter the homes of the betrayed traitors, seize them and lock them in the Church without food or water, where they were to beg for forgiveness. After three days Konrad entered the Church with his personal guard and spoke to each of the traitors before releasing them.

It was also during the twelfth month that communal dining halls were set up at each of the town gates. There, everyone could eat and drink, to the accompaniment of readings from the Holy

Book. Mr Snell was responsible for accounting and dispensing rations from the common store.

'You must realize there is no longer a distinction between yours and mine. Yours is mine,' was written up in large letters in each food hall.

28

'My friends!' rang Konrad's voice across the Square.

'What thing is of the greatest value?'

Silence.

'Is it not life itself? Life is the greatest treasure. That is what we compose songs about, what we attempt to capture in paintings, and it is essential we are clear on this point because once we are aware that we already possess the greatest treasure by simply being alive - we can create value! We know what is right and wrong. It is respectful of life and it enhances its dignity - do it! If it is not - don't do it, that is the only rule. And do we need The City to decide for us what is right and wrong?'

'No!' shouted the crowd in one voice.

'The time is upon us and we must Rejoice! Rejoice! Rejoice!'

A roar of approval echoed through the Square and across the plain.

'Joy is the core of your lives! Close your eyes, and do not open them until you feel it. A life of joy was Adam's original desire. If there is no joy in your body, if it has departed from your house, if you harbour feelings of hatred or contempt towards any of your fellow-citizens - you will be unhappy, and therefore you don't deserve to live in Aln.'

Konrad continued in this vein for some time, becoming harsher and increasingly agitated as he went on, before proposing another Edict.

'My friends, I must reveal to you a secret that you will find hard to accept. So onerous is the responsibility I bear that I perhaps should refrain from revealing it to you...'

'Tell us,' shouted the crowd fanatically.

'We must know.'

'Very well,' said Konrad. Slowly outstretching his arms, and with tears coursing down his cheeks, he declared for the first time, 'THERE IS NO NEW JERUSALEM! - IT DOES NOT EXIST!'

He might well have told them they had all suddenly died.

A horrible, loud groan escaped from the crowd, deep and trembling.

'It does not exist. All the money that you have sent, and your forefathers sent before you, never went further than The City. That is why The City is so wealthy! That is why The City exists! The City is corrupt! It is Hell! It is the place where fat rich priests preach to the thin hungry poor. The Electi have taken your money, earned by blood and sweat, and used it to ensure generations of their children will live in luxurious splendour long after you are dead and buried.'

Despair gripped the townspeople. They wailed, gnashed their teeth and shook their fists.

Gradually, the din subsided. One person noticed, then another, that Konrad was smiling. At this most terrible hour Konrad seemed to be pleased and cheerful.

'So, my friends, if New Jerusalem does not exist, it must be created. I therefore declare, in my capacity as Mayor of Aln, that Aln be considered New Jerusalem, and shall henceforth be known and function as such!'

Mr Snell then came forward with a parchment with the signatures of all the Burghers.

'A proclamation shall be issued throughout the Province that New Jerusalem has been established in the North-Western region and has declared war on The City! Prepare yourself for the Second Coming! Kneel down and pay obedience and rejoice!'

The Edict was passed instantly. Messengers were despatched with copies of the proclamation to every town in the region and Konrad wrote to the Electi. On receipt of Konrad's letter the Electi dismissed it as a hoax - publicly - and privately prepared to send in the troops.

On the third day of the first month, the Agents from The City who had come to collect the iron box containing the Aln Grand Donation were refused entry to the town. After repeated requests for admittance they were pelted from the walls with filth and offal. That, as far as The City was concerned, had been their last chance to negotiate. The Electi passed a motion that the insurrection at Aln was a major vacuum, and was to be dealt with as summarily and brutally as possible.

29

It had already been discussed at a Council Meeting, but it was Mr Farr who declared it had come to him in a dream that it should be done as soon as possible.

A day was appointed and arrangements began in earnest. Konrad had trained them well, they now understood that success lay in attending to the smallest details; it was usually the minutiae that Konrad would want to see before approving of any plan.

The Guild-Master Tailor and the Guild-Master Goldsmith were summoned to the Council Chamber to take measurements.

Mr Farr was in overall charge of the ceremony, and it was Mr Farr who declared to the assembled townspeople what had been revealed to him. The crowd knew it was a particularly important event because Konrad was also present, his appearances having been rare since the declaration of Aln as the New Jerusalem.

'We all know,' boomed Mr Farr, 'that our beloved Mayor is a Holy man. We know he is a Prophet. But now I can reveal that he has been appointed King of New Jerusalem! To him is given the crown and sceptre and throne until Isa shall descend and take it from him.'

The townspeople were absolutely astonished. They were attending a Coronation. Mr Map anointed Konrad's head with oil and handed him the sceptre, Mr Farr placed the crown on his head, and Mr Bull handed him the large sword with the words, 'Receive this Sword Of Justice, and therewith the power to bring all people of the Province under your authority.'

After this there was a long silence, as the significance of the occasion sank in, until Mr Farr urged them to join him in a hymn and they sang 'Lord of all he surveys'. Then Konrad addressed them.

'Friends! Subjects of New Jerusalem! I, like you, am a humble human being. However, Isa has seen fit, in his power and glory, to appoint a King to guard his earthly kingdom and prepare for his return. But I must tell you, my friends, I would rather tend the pigs than be King, but I must do what Isa has bade me do. Please understand there is no pleasure in it, for I am dead to the world of fleshy pleasure and profit. Any glory of me is therefore a reflection of the true glory of Him!'

There was a ripple of unease through the crowd and Konrad continued in anger, 'Shame on you to murmur against an ordinance of the Anointed One! If you were all to join together and oppose me I would still reign as King, because our Father would have it so!'

Konrad turned his back and stormed into the Council Chamber which Mr Farr declared was now to be known as the Royal Palace. The crowd was dispersed and they returned in silence to their homes.

For three days following the Coronation, Mr Map delivered one sermon after another, to ensure that the people understood that Konrad was the Messiah foretold in *The Teachings and Traditions of Isa,* and that his accession to the throne gave him jurisdiction not just over New Jerusalem but over the entire Province.

Though money had no function in New Jerusalem, the Mint-master was summoned to the Royal Palace and ordered to create an ornamental coinage, to celebrate the Coronation. On one side of the coin would be a profile of King Konrad, and on the other the inscription, 'One King over all'.

Magnificent robes had been made for the King by the Master-Tailor, trimmed with ermine and squirrel, and the golden crown was encrusted with precious stones from the common store. The Master-Goldsmith considered it his finest work. The sceptre was also rich in gold and stones and the royal sword was sheathed in a scabbard of silver with a heavy gold belt.

The entire Tailors' and Goldsmiths' Guild were busily employed for several weeks in attiring Konrad's numerous retinue on a corresponding scale of magnificence.

In the Square outside the Royal Palace a throne was erected, draped in a cloth of black and gold, where the King would sit to dispense Justice. Below the throne were built the benches where the Burghers, now called Royal Councillors, sat, and on either side the Royal Guard. A Royal Orator was appointed, Mr Farr, and he dealt with most of the minor ordinances and requests, such as for babies to be named by the King or the re-naming of streets.

Every day, it seemed the King's subjects were summoned to the Square to hear endless amendments to the Town Constitution, re-namings, or banished words.

And stories were travelling fast of the events in Aln.

'The poorest among them, who were once despised as beggars, now go around as finely dressed as the highest and most distinguished in The City.'

'Beggars have become as rich as Burghers, in fact richer.'

Such comments as these were made in every tavern in the Province by the envious and disgruntled. Aln was talked of in hope and awe, or in fear and anger, that was driving a wedge through the entire populace. Everyone had an opinion of the King, passionately for or against.

Swarms of the poor and disaffected swelled the roads to Aln in search of riches, revolution or salvation. After examination by the Royal Councillors some were admitted, and were very disappointed to find that although the King and his retinue lived in magnificent style, the mass of people had a rigorous ascetic discipline imposed on them. When it was explained to would-be refugees that whereas their Father permitted luxuries for the Messiah, he abominated superfluity in his subjects, they left in droves. A joke circulated that you had to be mad or a member for the Electi to gain access to Konrad's Kingdom. Not a few of those who were refused residency were indeed mad, but the majority of those in the small village that grew at the foot of the hill genuinely believed that their close proximity to the Holy City would protect them during the approaching Last Days.

The parlour of The Weavers' Arms was full. The fact that Aln was the Holy City didn't stop the regulars from enjoying their regular intake. Some, though, bewildered at why their town had been chosen by the Anointed One as his future home, were disconcerted by the dream-like atmosphere that enveloped them. Prophetic visions were now a daily occurrence.

Lumb the Butcher and Gregor the Candlemaker were having a heated debate about it.

'Why not The City then? I mean you'd think it was better, with its size and all.'

'But it wasn't written that the rich would inherit the Kingdom, was it?'

'He's right, it's not written,' snorted Kitty.

'And isn't it the peasants and the artisans who have accepted the true word? It was prophesied that it was from their ranks that the true followers would appear. It stands to reason.'

'Well spoken,' said Konrad from the doorway, 'Kitty, I'll have a glass of your best and the same for everyone in the parlour.'

No one moved a muscle. Everywhere the King of New Jerusalem was greeted with great enthusiasm. Women distinguished themselves by the ardour of their loyalty, but here was something radical - the King in his scholar's garb, without a Guard, as though he was the Schoolmaster again, as though it had all been a dream. It didn't seem right to them, the King in a tavern with ordinary people.

'Don't be frightened,' said Konrad, 'I might be a King, but I still need good company and the odd glass.'

The drinkers tried not to be frightened as the King had

ordered, each one wanting to leave and knowing that it was impossible.

'Please carry on with your discussion, don't mind me,' said Konrad cheerfully. Conversation resumed, in a most unnatural manner. In theory, anyone could say anything, for taverns were for free speech and debate, but who was about to argue with the King?

'Yes...well, as I was saying,' said Lumb the Butcher, with a dry mouth, 'there was never any possibility of The City becoming...' Konrad sidled up to the Butcher, his head cocked to one side to listen intently.

'Please, continue,' he urged the Butcher, but it was impossible for him. He could only smile inanely with awe. It was the same throughout the evening. Konrad killed every conversation he attempted to join. Finally, he had had enough.

'Gentlemen, since you find my presence so irksome I will talk to you. You have it all wrong, you are confused because previously those in authority were to be detested. But you do not hate me, do you?'

There were loud denials of this idea and confirmations of devotion.

'You give us what we want,' said one.

'Exactly. But you cannot forsake your old ways. Your minds are plodding the ancient furrows like lumbering oxen, and that will not do at all. You are still thinking and behaving like slaves.'

'We love you,' said another.

'And that I appreciate, but you must grasp that I am merely your servant. You must not feel that you are below me, holding me afloat. It is the very opposite, I am at the bottom holding you all up like Atlas.'

'What happens when The City sends troops?' asked one.

'Ah...is that all you are worried about? Yes, they will send troops against us, of that there can be no doubt. But they will not win against me. I have a power within me that can never be crushed. Trying to kill me would be like trying to kill the sun.

Another question, ask me anything.'

'We miss our children. Tell us how they are.'

'They are thriving, there is nothing to worry about, they are in excellent condition, it is for them that we must be strong. They will not remember the Old World but only New Jerusalem. They will not know greed, envy or hatred. They will develop into pure adults if they are trained to be pure children.'

'Do they speak of us?'

'Yes, they do,' Konrad laughed, 'They haven't forgotten their parents, but they also well understand that they are pioneers. Any pain they suffer is a small price to pay for a world they will inherit. Nothing can compare to the satisfaction they feel. Please learn from them and feel the same.'

As the drinkers relaxed, the questions followed thick and fast and an almost natural atmosphere prevailed.

'What happens if there is a theft from the common storehouse? How would you respond?'

'If such a terrible thing should occur I would dispense Justice in the most appropriate manner. You must also realize that whereas in the past a thief might conceal his crime, where will he run to now?'

No one had considered this, where indeed?

'There will be precious little mercy for those who leave New Jerusalem before Isa comes. Please do not forget that within these walls we are safe. Outside them, the unbelievers will suffer indescribable tortures. In short, anyone leaving here will be cut to pieces by devils and forfeit his everlasting happiness in Paradise.'

Konrad rose to his feet. His gracefulness seemed now, not an affectation of a City man, but an attribute of the inherent dignity of a King.

'I have enjoyed our little chat, I hope you have too?'

All nodded unreservedly.

'Until next time then.'

When Konrad had gone, everyone let out a deep sigh of relief.

Konrad wandered through the narrow streets, keeping

himself well-hidden in the shadows, observing domestic scenes through the shutters, until he arrived back at the Palace.

Later that night he was awoken by shouts and torchlight in the Square below. Julius hammered at his door frantically until he answered.

'What is it, Julius?' Konrad asked calmly.

'My King, the Last Days have come - there are fires in the sky!'

'Calm down Julius, explain.'

'First there was one, then many appeared. Could it be Isa's chariot?'

'Do not fear,' said Konrad smiling, 'Go into the Square and tell those gathered it is a sign that Isa is watching over the Kingdom, then come back here.'

Konrad dressed hurriedly and rushed to the watchtower to obtain a better view. In the distance were the watch-fires of the enemy. Because they had set up camp in the mountains and over the horizon, they appeared to be in the sky.

'So it begins,' said Konrad to the night-watchman.

Later, as the sun was rising, Konrad and Julius had a strange conversation that troubled Julius for some time. Konrad was sitting at the window looking through a telescope at The City's forces setting up their advance camp. Julius stood behind him and murmured a well-known proverb that seemed appropriate but which seemed to annoy Konrad. What he said was, 'Peace is harder to win than a battle.'

'Sentiment outlives itself, Julius,' responded Konrad, 'That proverb you repeat mechanically has no living meaning to you. You picked it up from somewhere and adopted it with no thought of its true interpretation.'

'My Father used it when there was an argument in the house.'

'Ah, and did you know that proverbs make you blind?'

'Blind?'

'They confuse believing with doing.'

'Don't they remind us of what we wish for?'

'Do they? - they stop our thoughts emerging. When a principle is generally agreed upon complacency takes hold and that principle has then lost the power to stimulate action.'

'I'm confused.'

'Think over what you yourself said.'

'Peace...is harder to win....than a battle. I can't see what's wrong with that.'

'No one would disagree with you while never experiencing what it means, the principle in question - Peace! Nothing will be done because it is agreed that it is true. It means nothing personally unless you have come to your own conclusion. It becomes an abstract. It is not perceived as a personal matter, it becomes a truth and not a responsibility. Peace is not the absence of war, anyhow.'

'I'm sorry, Sir.'

'So you should be, for repeating such a proverb prevents you from thinking and reneges responsibility for what is about to happen to our Kingdom. Julius, you must understand that it is far easier for the Electi to protect the Province by force than it is for an ordinary person such as yourself to bring about a change of heart.'

'But the purpose of the Electi should be to protect the ordinary person?'

'Only if you believe the Electi exist. The genius of the Electi is that they have persuaded you that the Electi is a group of special people. They are the Electi because they have told you so, not because they have special qualities of compassion for ordinary citizens. That is their doctrine - the Electi and the mundane.'

'But quality is essential, that is what you have taught me.'

'There you go again! Only those who are able to regenerate themselves, are able to rise to the surface. Those able to master their minds. It is not praising Justice that produces change - that is primitive - but to regenerate the mind of one individual will send currents of change throughout the Province, without a single word being spoken or a blow struck. That is the secret weapon of the Electi!'

31

Later that morning, heralded by three blasts from the Trumpets of Jericho, the citizens saw the King enter Mount Zion, formerly known as the Square.

The King had been preceded by the Master of Ceremonies, Mr Snell, with a white staff in his hand. The King, attired in his royal garments, holding the sceptre, the royal crown on his head, was riding on a white horse. On either side of him rode two pages, one holding aloft the Holy Book, the other the Sword of Justice in its silver scabbard. Behind him was a long procession headed by the Royal Councillors, also on horseback, then attendants, then servants of the Royal Household. The whole procession was flanked by the Royal Guard who surrounded the King when he took his throne for the proceedings.

When the King sat, the Court was seated, and all waited.

'I have summoned you this morning for two important reasons,' said the King. 'The first is to tell you that sexual intercourse must not, under any circumstances, be considered sinful. Neither is it a sin to be naked like Adam and Eve, rather it is a true expression of innocence and purity.'

The townspeople listened in utter silence.

'Furthermore, I have decided to re-introduce polygamy. Isa's precept to increase and multiply must be our guide. The Patriarchs of the Holy Land have given us the example. Polygamy must be restored to New Jerusalem. All previous marriage vows are null and void, though of course some of you may wish to re-marry your former wives. From now on, all that is needed to marry is the joining of hands, and the words "I take thee." A divorce may be effected by the joining of hands, and the words, "I renounce thee." Any sign of disaffection will be regarded as treason and duly punished.'

At once a group of women, among some of the King's most ardent supporters, tore off their clothes and began a whirling dance in ecstasy.

'Father! Father! Father! Give! Give! Give!,' they screamed repeatedly, holding their palms aloft towards the sky. Others followed, until a great expanse of flesh was exposed in the Square.

Konrad turned to look at Mr Farr, and noticed his lips were pursed.

'The second thing of importance I must tell you,' continued Konrad above the chaotic licence, 'is that this morning a letter arrived from the Electi calling for us to surrender.'

Konrad jumped to his feet and shouted at the cavorting crowd.

'I have replied - telling them that we will fight for truth with our last breath.'

When he glanced again to his right, he saw Mr Farr disappearing among the naked crowd.

32

'One hour before the visit,' said Julius, consulting the Schoolhouse clock.

Though unforeseen forces were gathering outside the walls, those inside felt secure, and no more so than the children, deep within the labyrinthine Royal Palace. Throughout the time of the Accession the children continued their studies undisturbed. It might be thought that such a sultry atmosphere of confinement would have produced a great deal of friction and frequent eruptions of tension, but this was far from true. For one thing, they had more space than their parents imagined and luxurious surroundings. The outside of the Council Chamber looked like any other municipal building, large but not grand, but what was not generally known was that two unseen thirds of it were below ground-level, cut into the rock. Even Konrad had not explored all the rooms. To the children, the honeycomb of corridors and chambers was a town within a town, an inner Kingdom within the inner sanctum of the Province. Some of the youngest were finding it difficult to remember what the outside looked like, and life before Konrad was very vague. They never complained, they ate well, exercised, and apart from the whiteness of their skin they were remarkably healthy.

Konrad was the only bridge between the two worlds. Occasionally, Julius ushered the children onto the roof to witness the King pass an Edict in the Square below, but only as a reward for their progress. And how alien the world and the people seemed to them, how primitive!

'I wonder how the King can bear it?' said one; the others giggled.

They were articulate beyond their years, enjoying erudite

119

discussions, but retained the child's vulnerability and need for comfort.

They could hardly believe that the scenes below had any concern for them. Their daily routine was this: Julius woke them at six o'clock by ringing a bell in the dormitory. Later on, some of the older children were given their own rooms. After ablutions they made their way to the Refectory where, usually, Konrad would be waiting for them. While breakfasting, passages would be read from 'The Teachings of King Konrad,' with children taking it in turns, followed by a question and answer session and a short discussion. After breakfast Konrad would ask Julius to bring certain children to his study. While others attended their classes, these selected children were given certain tasks, to research a topic in the Archive, or compile a short essay on a specific subject. Some might be reprimanded.

About two days before Konrad chose his first wife, two boys were summoned, and being two of the brightest pupils, assumed they would be given a subject to research. They had no inkling of what was to happen.

'Please be seated, Gentlemen,' said Konrad, pacing up and down his study, his hands together at his chest as though in prayer. He always wore his habitual black when inside the Palace, only donning the regalia on State occasions.

'Perhaps you can tell me, what are the indispensable attributes of a Gentleman?'

His voice was sweet and deep as always, yet the boys could detect in his tone a trace of fury at variance with his manner.

'Tolerance,' said one.

'Honesty,' said the other.

'Without doubt two essential requirements, but there is still one yet greater, more vital, without which there can be no ascent of character, for it is the very foundation on which the perfect Gentleman is built and that is - Humility!'

Both boys flushed deeply. Their behaviour of late had been sadly lacking in this quality.

'The humility I speak of is born out of privilege and a

profound sense of responsibility. Without it we are animals. Now you may think that when I am the King before my subjects I could not possibly be considered to be in a humble position. You may, in fact, be already dreaming of achieving high standing in the Province and lording it over your fellows, but, there lies your downfall. I am a servant!...I would go as far as to say I am a King because my heart is the humblest in the Province!'

Looking at Konrad in full flow, his large bright eyes aglow, his perfect teeth and full lips, such a noble being seemed anything but a servant - a servant of Isa, perhaps? The blood of a King and the blood of a Prophet intermingled in his veins, the most perfect being the boys could imagine.

'I will, Gentlemen, give you the benefit of the doubt and illustrate the kind of Gentleman I expect you to become, with a story from my past. Experience is after all far superior to theory, is it not? Experience is power.'

Listening to one of the King's personal experiences was one of the children's greatest tasks. Konrad's stories from his past were to be memorized verbatim. They reverberated with meaning long after first hearing; resonances came echoing back, creating further meanings months later. The boys settled into their seats with delicious anticipation.

'Once, when I was a young boy, I was sent to stay with an uncle in the mountains. After some days at my uncle's house there was a very heavy fall of snow and all work stopped in the village and the fields. We children rushed out, of course, to play in the snow. Icicles were hanging from the trees and every house had smoke coming from its chimney. The pond was frozen over and was too tempting for us to resist, and we walked on it, and no doubt wanting to impress the girls, some of us bolder ones ventured out into the middle of the pond where the ice was thinner, where the fish could be seen moving sluggishly under our feet. It was pure happiness and joy, until, without warning, and to our great horror, there was a loud cracking sound, the ice opened and five boys, including me, were plunged into the freezing water. There was no doubt about it, without help we would be unable to scramble through the cracks and we were either going to drown or freeze to death.'

Konrad paused to take a sip of coffee and light a taper. The boys gazed at him, their mouths open.

'Eventually, the rescuers arrived with hooks and ropes, but the work was slow, the ice was still moving and groaning, and to make matters worse it had begun to snow again. I looked at one of my companions, who was the weakling among us, and he was turning blue. But then, and I know I didn't imagine it, he winked at me, and smiled. He actually grinned and winked as if to say, "Don't worry, you will come to no harm." Meanwhile, the rescuers raced against our death, moving slowly closer with their ropes, testing every inch of the ice with their weight before moving towards us. They reached my friend first, my friend who had winked encouragement, but he refused to take the rope and instead offered it to another, who was very distressed, and he was hauled away to safety. Then he directed the rescuers to another whose head was periodically slipping under the water, then another until finally he gave the rope to me. He waited his turn to be rescued, the last one. Unfortunately, he could wait no longer; he succumbed to the cold, and died.'

The two boys wept openly, struck by the boy's fate.

'When they finally pulled him out there was the faintest trace of a smile on his blue lips. On questioning my fellow-survivors I found that he had swum to each of us and each had received a smile and a wink.

'When the young man's deeds were reported in the village, people wept and his name is still spoken with reverence to this day. He was a true Gentleman, giving up his life in the way of the Gentleman. And that, I feel, eloquently embodies the spirit of what I hope you will aspire to from this moment on. Such people are the élite of humanity. I have noticed that among your ranks there is emerging a contemptible tendency to ally oneself with authority, without any conviction of one's own. This contributes to the devaluation of your humanity and therefore your right to be considered leaders. I have assumed leadership of you only to reveal your wisdom...is that clear?'

'Yes, Sir,' the boys chimed, severely chastened.

'You are dismissed, Gentlemen.'

After a light repast at noon, the children spent the afternoon in recreational pursuits. At seven o'clock, each child joined a small discussion group. This was one of Konrad's most successful experiments. It was his intention to try it out on the whole population eventually. Each child was assigned to a group of five, each group had a leader who met with Julius beforehand to be briefed on the theme of the meeting and be given appropriate reading material and the main points to be covered. After the meetings were over the leaders met Julius again to report in detail on how each group had progressed and the conclusions reached, or not. These reports were then handed in to Konrad at the end of each day. Every Monday the children were re-assigned to another group though the group leaders usually remained the same. Konrad placed great importance on the group meeting, seeing it as a basic building block to producing self-motivated citizens for New Jerusalem. He took a keen interest in the flow of discussion. From Julius' reports he noted the unique diversity of opinions and charted the slow but steady development of each pupil on a graph. After some time, patterns had begun to emerge, divergences of opinion arrived at the same conclusion after a torturous exploration.

'The discussion meeting is where a perfect self-regulated world can be created in miniature, where every difference can be overcome through dialogue,' Konrad told Julius, who had been doubtful at first of allowing unsupervised discussion.

'Each child must think for itself and must be quite used to open and spontaneous dialogue. That way they will become able to search for every solution within its own sphere of resource; Konrad assured him.

'Imagine, Julius, the whole City, each man, woman and child discussing and debating passionately topics vital to all! True democracy, Julius!'

At first the subjects had been a little too cerebral. One of the earliest was the correlation of Aristotle's *Ethics,* Plato's Utopia and Plotinus. Konrad eagerly charted the flow and connection of ideas, compiling what he referred to as a 'map of ideas,' until late into the night. But after a while it struck him forcibly that how an idea was expressed was as important as the thought itself, and that the discussion meeting was in itself far more influential on the daily development of the children. He realized that the children had grown adept at theorising but not at communicating. The true value of each meeting therefore was that no aphorisms be allowed to form. The challenge of having to communicate with others, whom they might normally avoid, was affecting them greatly. The subjects for discussion were to be merely the means by which the children extended their ability to transcend difference.

Konrad became greatly excited by the results of his search to create true leaders.

One day, Julius came to him in despair over an argument he had had with a pupil.

'He is not capable,' he complained, 'he's cheeky, insubordinate, and arrogant.'

'I disagree,' said Konrad, 'you are judging others according to your own standards. You are a methodical and analytical person. Therefore you value only those who are too. You regard only those who have the same tendencies as being capable. If you become absorbed in your own self-importance you will be unable to appreciate the qualities of a person different from you, you will only see their faults.'

Julius was crestfallen. He had forgotten the golden rule, 'Look for the solution inside yourself.'

'Your development depends on whether you can see his strong points and polish them. They are all diamonds that just need polishing Julius, that is all...'

He squeezed Julius' shoulder firmly.

'It requires a diamond to polish a diamond.'

33

In defiance of the rule of communality, Mr Farr invited Mr Bull for dinner. Mr Bull accepted unhesitatingly, he missed so much the pleasure of an intimate dinner party like the good old days. As it was, he found it very difficult to swallow his food while sharing a table with peasants who a few months previously had been in his service. Mr Bull was one of those middle-aged businessmen who had dreamed of purchasing a villa in the South in which to spend his winter months; no chance of that now.

'This is now clearly impossible,' said Mr Bull regretfully, 'not that I'm complaining, mind you.'

'No, of course not,' said Mr Farr. 'His will be done.'

'But you must admit, I do look a little ridiculous dressed in this fustian cloth.'

The two Royal Councillors giggled conspiratorially.

'More potato?' asked Mr Farr.

Ever since he had officiated at the Coronation, Mr Farr had grown increasingly dissatisfied. Before Konrad had come to them he had constantly complained how little time he had to catch up on his reading or to familiarize himself with the current ideas of the Electi. Now he had all the time he could have wished for, and was at war with them. Apart from his minor duties at the Court and the occasional public announcement, he could spend the best part of the day engrossed in the King's magnificent library, if he wanted to.

'Not that I'm complaining, you understand,' he explained, 'but I realize now that I gained pleasure from my reading because I looked forward to the precious moments I could spare for it. With so much time at my disposal the pleasure has evaporated.' Mr Bull nodded vigorously.

'I know exactly how you feel, Mr Farr. After the Polygamy Edict I was very anxious to comply with the King's wishes, but now, with three wives, it is not as pleasurable as I imagined. I didn't realize how content I was as a widower. I did what I wanted to do when I wanted to do it, and now, for the sake of...'

'Momentary pleasure, Mr Bull, transient as the dew.'

'Exactly. I think not less than many have found that desires hatched in the mind are not what's required when translated into reality.'

'I couldn't agree more, Mr Bull, I couldn't, and talking about reality, The City troops are gathering every day. I should think we have two weeks at the very least before they attack.'

'Do you think they'd be so foolish?'

'Foolish, you say!...Well, that's one word you could use for it, but there will be hardship -'

'But they will lose, Mr Farr, you must believe that?'

Mr Farr hesitated for some moments, poured himself and Mr Bull more wine, and lowered his voice.

'Our ancestors saw to it that Aln -' Mr Bull started at the use of that name and coughed loudly.

'I'm sorry, New Jerusalem, was built to withstand any possible attack. The walls are unbreachable, the slopes too steep for -'

'- Too steep for what, Mr Farr?'

'Too steep for siege machines.'

'Ah, it is not the battle you fear but the siege that may follow?'

'But, Mr Bull, don't you see that The City can never ultimately lose?'

'Against the Anointed One!'

'They will starve us into submission, however long it takes.'

'You are forgetting one thing, Mr Farr - our King! Our King is divinely appointed. Our Father will not sit by and watch the King defeated by his enemies. He will protect us.'

'The resources of The City are infinite.'

'Are not the Anointed One's?'

Mr Farr became pensive and began pacing the room. He looked out through the shutters and smiled wanly, then said in a whisper, 'Mr Bull. I must swear you to the utmost secrecy.'

'We are old friends, is there any need to -'

'My old friend, if my memory serves me right, as a great philosopher said, "All things must pass."'

Mr Bull stared at Mr Farr.

'Do you mean -'

'I mean trifles that I prized highly as a child, I disregarded as a man.'

'But...'

'These honey-coloured rocks will be here long after my flesh is part of the hillside.'

'I don't think I want -'

'There are others, Mr Bull.'

'Others?'

'There are others who are of the same mind. Others who might have a certain scepticism in regard to -'

'The worm in the bowels of the lion?' said Mr Bull indignantly.

'Who possess a certain healthy scepticism, that's what I mean...the forces are gathering outside our town, Mr Bull. Our home. They might greatly appreciate a little help from within these walls?'

'Who are the others?'

'Ah well, that's difficult to say.'

'Difficult to say?'

'As difficult as it is to test your sympathies.'

'My sympathies lie with the Anointed One.'

'So do mine.'

'Rely on the Messiah said -'

'Indeed, and his Prophet?...or should I say perhaps, his false -'

'Mr Farr!' shouted Mr Bull, spilling his wine and jumping to his feet.

'We'll talk - we'll talk further on the matter, Mr Farr, but now I really must, rather tired and all that, must go back to the wife - wives, you know -'

'Of course, Mr Bull, until then.'

When Mr Bull had been gone some minutes Mr Farr looked through the shutters once more.

'Damn, damn, damn,' he said quietly.

The grille in the door of the Royal Palace slammed open.

'It's late,' said an unseen mouth.

'It's important. The king is expecting me to report.'

'The password?'

'Judas.'

The night-watchman unbolted the door and admitted a Royal Councillor.

34

Shortly before his marriage to Mr Flagg's widow, and fourteen of her young friends, the King held a court of Justice in the Square.

Far from decreasing, the number of grievances among the citizens was increasing. Everyone had equal shares in all property, no one but the King had any dealings with money, any man could take any woman for a wife, there was no work, and yet dissatisfaction was spreading. The King was not in a good mood.

The whole Court was in attendance, all dressed in mulberry velvet. When it was time for the King to address the assembly there was not a sound. He rose from his throne and surveyed the upturned faces. The King was angry, but as usual, his manner was at variance with his true feelings.

'Complaints are a sign of weak faith,' he began.

'Complaints are cowardly, base, an abomination. Complaints are passive, they offer no solution but point to the weaknesses in others. Complaints are a sign that a person has stopped re-generating themselves. That person's mind is stagnant.'

In the middle of this discourse Mr Bull burst away from the Councillors' benches crying, 'Holy! Holy! Holy! is the King, and holy are his people!'

He repeated these words as a chant and began to dance in front of the throne. The crowd watched in silence and the guard gripped their pikes tightly, as Mr Bull danced in ever-decreasing circles, his hair floating in the wind and his fleshy partly-clothed body quivering with tiny convulsions, came to a halt.

'It has been revealed to me,' cried Mr Bull breathlessly, 'that I must play the part of the Court Fool.'

He then skipped and leapt in imitation of the antics of a

fool, prostrating himself, throwing various grotesque poses, gesticulating wildly like a demented gargoyle. He continued this crazy dance until he fell exhausted. Then he looked up a woman's skirt and giggled, rolling over and over on the cobbles. Then, rising to his feet with difficulty, he declared that the Holy Spirit had been through him, and attempted to kiss embarrassed bystanders on the lips. The King, who up until that point had been sternly silent, descended the dais and walked towards Mr Bull as though to comfort him, stopping his Guard accompanying him into the crowd. But when Mr Bull saw the King walking towards him he skipped and jumped away and before anyone could stop him, seated himself on the throne and said in a venomous hiss, 'It is I who by right should be King here, since it is I who has made you what you are.'

With a nod from the King, Mr Bull was easily overpowered and dragged screaming from the Square, kicking out at bystanders within reach and attempting to bite the Guards.

The King addressed his people, asking them not to heed what Mr Bull had said because he was not in his right mind. The session was then hastily called to a close with a minimum of ceremony. The King, enraged, had Mr Bull arrested and incarcerated in the Palace dungeon where he remained for three days. After he begged for forgiveness, claiming he had been beguiled by devils and could not therefore be held responsible, he was released with no charge and the King's personal Guard was doubled.

To celebrate the King's wedding a banquet was held in the Square, with music, song and dance, and some of his favourite passages from the Holy Book read out. After it turned dark, the King and his new wives retired to the Palace with his Guard and a selection of respectable townspeople, where the drinking and the entertainment continued. The King was in high spirits, until that is Mr Bull burst in on the party, drunk and carrying a musket.

The King, who had been serving his guests with his own hand, put down the jug of wine and addressed the distraught Mr Bull calmly. 'Welcome, Mr Bull. I had not seen fit to invite you, but since you seem anxious to attend our little gathering, please -'

'Shut up, Konrad,' said Mr Bull, crying.

The King smiled and, turning to his Guard, said, 'Don't worry, he won't harm us.' His voice was gentle, without the slightest trace of fear or surprise.

'Won't I?' cried Mr Bull, 'it's you I've come for, Konrad, I've come to put an early end to your reign.'

'Come, my friend, you're upset, fearful of the gathering armies perhaps?'

'There's only one thing we need be fearful of and I've a loaded musket pointed at it right now.'

The horrified guests could never have anticipated what happened next.

The King walked to the centre of the refectory, his eyes never leaving Mr Bull's, who said, 'I know what you're doing, Konrad, but you won't succeed. You're flesh and blood like the rest of us. A bullet will pass through you like piss through snow.'

Mr Bull was sweating profusely, blinking and looking around. Then the King unbuttoned his mulberry jacket, then his waistcoat, and bared his breast.

'Come closer, Mr Bull, I will not resist.'

'I know who you are, Konrad, and what you are doing.'

'Do you, indeed?'

Mr Bull staggered towards the King, and though he had a loaded musket he was the more frightened.

'Damn you, Konrad. Damn you!'

'Do not be frightened, Mr Bull. You have the opportunity of only one shot when killing a King.'

Mr Bull stalked Konrad as though he were an unpredictable wild beast.

'Shut up, you lump of devil shit!'

'Oh come, Mr Bull, no need for foul language on such an occasion. After all, you are about to become infamous.'

Although his guests were frightened, the King's extraordinary confidence convinced them no harm would befall them, but the King? The musket barrel was within an inch of the King's chest.

'Stop looking at me,' screamed Mr Bull.

Mr Bull's finger pulled the trigger.

There was a click, then Mr Bull fainted.

The firearm had refused to go off.

The King laughed, genuinely amused. Mr Bull was seized by the Guard and dragged away. For some moments the guests assumed that the whole episode had been a piece of play-acting stage-managed by the King to intimidate his detractors. The King resumed serving the wine as though it had been.

But it was not. When the captain of the Guard examined the musket he found to his horror that it was in fact loaded. Aiming at the fireplace, he discharged the ball perfectly well. There was no mechanical reason why the musket had not fired the first time. There was no explanation for what happened.

The King spent the rest of the night dancing with each of his wives until dawn. New Jerusalem had received its first miracle.

35

The next evening, the houses of Mr Bull, Mr Map, and several other secret enemies were broken into and they were dragged from their beds to the Palace Dungeon. The majority of the population were silent on the matter, while a minority gave vent to murmurs of dissent.

In the morning the trumpet was sounded for a call to repentance, when Mr Farr invited questions from the assembly on the matter of the arrests.

'They are being questioned at this very moment. Next!'

'And what will happen to them?'

'That is for the King to decide. Next!'

'Where is the King?'

'Aye, why isn't he talking to us instead of sending his monkey?'

'You must remember,' continued Mr Farr unperturbed, 'the King is on his honeymoon. Since he cannot go out of the Walls of the Holy City, because he would be arrested by the devil's legions, he has retired for three days from public duties, to enjoy his new status with his wives.'

No one responded to this; fair was fair.

'I'm sure you wouldn't deny the King time to enjoy his conjugal rights?'

This caused a great deal of sniggering and whispers. Someone shouted, 'Good luck to the King!', and 'May the King enjoy his conjugal rights!'

The citizens were dispersed to continue work on the defences.

Later that day, Mr Bull, Mr Map and several others were fastened with iron bands around their necks to the lime-trees in the Church Close. There they remained for the remainder of the King's honeymoon, without food or water, or sympathy. They made no attempt to plead their case, or even talk among themselves. With no provision for their bodily functions, their humiliation was complete.

On the fourth day after the arrests, the throne was draped in a black cloth and as the people rushed to the assembly at the sound of the trumpet, they saw the King already seated waiting for them.

Mr Farr, with great solemnity, appeared from the Palace holding aloft the Sword of Justice.

He began to speak and the crowd fell silent.

'It has been decided, on the evidence given to us and the confessions of the prisoners themselves, that the heaviest sentence must be administered. They have committed crimes against Isa and his Prophet, the King. We cannot allow them to live.'

With this, a signal was given, the prisoners were brought, bound and gagged, before the throne and made to kneel.

'Your crimes would put Judas to shame,' said Konrad. 'You plotted to bring down New Jerusalem and you must pay the heaviest price.'

Mr Map began to blubber incoherently.

Konrad took the sword from Mr Farr and walked down among the crowd.

'Who will do the Messiah's work?' he shouted, offering the Sword of Justice to anyone who would use it.

'Who would rid the Kingdom of its traitors?'

No one so much as twitched, they were too mesmerized by the close proximity of the King, unsure of his true intention. They would wait and see.

'Is there no one who will help me?'

'I will,' said Gammy, breaking through to Konrad and hopping into the circle where the King stood.

'Bless you, Gammy. Gammy the Innocent you shall be

134

called by future generations, and your name shall be revered as one who had true faith.'

Gammy smiled his toothy grin, nodding his head at the crowd.

'You have proved your loyalty, but it is not for you to spill blood. Since execution is the lowest job of all it is fitting that it should be done by the King!'

With that, the King walked purposefully to the first prisoner in the line, Mr Map, and raised the sword above his head. There was a loud intake of breath, a terrible and beautiful moment of Justice.

But as the sword whistled down it missed the neck of Mr Map and raised sparks from the cobbles. The king cast aside the sword and stalked back to the throne, his head bowed. At once everyone understood what had happened.

'How could you?' asked the King dejectedly.

'After all I have done to free you. Do you really think I would kill a subject? Do you not understand Justice? I came to free you not to bind you in chains. You would have watched me kill one of your fellow-citizens!'

The citizens were overcome with shame. All heads were bowed.

'There will be no executions in New Jerusalem. The life of the King and the life of the beggar are of equal value.'

The King summoned Gammy, and placed his hand on his head affectionately.

'I am equal to Gammy. Our functions are different, of course. Gammy could never achieve what I can, and I can never see what Gammy sees. This does not make his life less than mine. This is what I have taught you until my mouth is dry and yet you do nothing. Perhaps it would be better if I abdicated in favour of a less exacting ruler?'

A murmur brewed in the crowd that grew into a roar of acclamation. Men fell on their knees and begged him to stay. There were cries of, 'Isa protect King Konrad!' and, 'Do not leave the divine King!' Even the prisoners raised their heads and implored the King to remain, and begged his forgiveness and pledged loyalty for the rest of their lives.

That was how the King was confirmed in his role, by a kind of popular election.

The next morning, Mr Bull, Mr Map and the other prisoners were ejected from the Holy City. They begged to see the King once more, but there was no reply from the Royal Palace. They were each given a square of white linen to wave at the enemy, some food, and a commemorative coin.

Far from being cut to pieces by the City freelances, they were welcomed. They were given wine and tents to rest in and afterwards questioned most politely as to the condition of the town's stores and defences. This the prisoners were only too glad to do. Mr Bull even undertook to make a list of enemies the King still had in Aln, and to make contact with them, for a stipulated sum of money. How he was going to do this was not clear.

After the Captain of the freelances was sure he had gained all the information he thought useful, all the prisoners were beheaded, and their bodies dumped in the sewerage pit.

36

The Battle of Aln was fought on the sixteenth day of the sixth month.

The time of year should have ensured the conditions were hot and dry, but they were not. The dark clouds and a rise in the temperature at dawn were taken as a bad sign by the freelances. The air was thick and moist, the light thin.

At sunrise the Captain had ridden up to the town gates and shouted out a formal summons to surrender. He stated that neither the Kingdom nor its King was recognized by the Electi, and that a Council of War had been formed to wage war against the insurgents of Aln and bring them into submission. Then he added, 'I am empowered by the Electi to offer every citizen of Aln an amnesty. All except the so-called King and his immediate Councillors and remaining Burghers.'

After a considerable time, the great doors were opened, and there, standing with his legs astride, hands on hips, looking every inch the King, was Konrad dressed in half-armour.

'You are declaring war on New Jerusalem, Captain. You will therefore suffer defeat.'

The Captain steadied his horse, to take a good look at the man he had heard so much about. He was impressed with the King's regal bearing. He could see no one else in the streets. There was a complete silence.

'That is not for me to decide,' the Captain replied. 'Our Father will decide for us both. I am here to offer the citizens their freedom and their lives.'

'You are merely fulfilling a role, like an actor in a pageant, the same role played by the occupying army that executed Isa. Only the age is different. You will not succeed this time.'

'Since you are clearly a madman I refuse to continue bantering with you.'

'Is the Prophet of Isa a madman?'

'I give you one hour in which to surrender the town. If you do not comply, the amnesty will be withdrawn and the battle will commence, a battle which you cannot hope to win...do you wish to make a reply?'

'I have spoken,' said the King.

When the designated hour was up, the sky was a grey-green and it seemed more like a gloomy day in the eleventh month than the height of summer.

All was ready and all were waiting within the walls of the Holy City for the King to do something. However, when the main body of the freelances emerged from the mountains it was soon realized that they had been fooled into thinking that the advance camp had been the entire force. Only the King seemed unafraid. The lances were so numerous, and so tightly packed together were the foot-soldiers, that their movement resembled the wind moving through corn. There was no doubting now The City's serious intent. Mr Farr stared with an open mouth.

'Do not worry, Mr Farr,' said the King quietly. They were standing in the Church tower, the highest point in the town. Down below, the plain seemed to have grown soldiers.

'They have brought numbers to frighten us, but you see the yellow tunics?'

Mr Farr's lips moved together but failed to form a word.

'Most of those men are mercenaries, not fighting for a cause but for money. They are no better at fighting than we are, and we have the greatest possible cause!'

There was a tremendous amount of activity taking place on the lower slopes as the freelances hauled their machines of war over the rocks and crevices.

'First they will bombard us, perhaps for several days, then

stage an attack, but they will not breach these walls. They will hope to frighten us, but it will be like a frog increasing its size to frighten a lion. They are not of one mind.'

'Are they not?' asked Mr Farr weakly.

'No. Even a person at cross-purposes with himself is bound to fail. They are divided in spirit so numbers are of no account. We are few, but our victory is certain.'

'Why?'

'Because we do not seek to kill anyone, and because we are right.'

'May the faith of this town withstand this onslaught!'

'It'll stand, should the onslaught last a thousand days.'

Amongst the baggage trains that accompanied the army was a banner depicting the Virgin and Child on a gold ground.

'Isa help us,' said Mr Farr, when the King was out of earshot.

Four hundred horsemen were counted. Behind them came two hundred crossbow men and fifty handgunners. Next came the wagon carrying a cross and a priest, followed by smiths, leather-workers, armourers, pike-makers, tailors, powder and lead and twenty wagons of arrows. Then came the cannon and sundry equipment. There were wagons bulging with cow-hides for the stables and tents and corn for at least twelve weeks. There were ninety head of oxen, nine-hundred-weight of lard, 1,200 pieces of cheese, 80 tubs of salted fish, 56 pounds of uncut candles, vinegar, oil, pepper, saffron and ginger, two tons of Southern wine, and 158 barrels of beer. The number of freelances was too numerous to be counted. Mr Farr sent instructions to the Royal Defenders of the ramparts and the watchtowers, to remain silent on the scale of the assault for as long as possible.

Three hours of cannonade hardly caused a crack in the southern wall. At midday an attack was opened along the whole line.

At first the forces succeeded in making some ground as a small party pressed beyond the outer line of fortifications, their aim being to secure a path for the cannon to be able to reach closer. Wave upon wave of the freelances repeatedly attacked the gates but with no result. Their attempt to place scaling ladders was also futile. The defenders were well-prepared in the ramparts, with heavy stones, boiling tar and quicklime, which were hurled down on the heads of the attackers, leaving many dead or fatally wounded. Confusion soon disrupted the spiritless mercenaries. As the King had predicted, they would not be so free and easy with their lives again.

At three o'clock it began to rain, heavily at first, then torrentially. The confusion increased, the attack was turning into a huge disaster as the freelances slipped in the mud and sand of the slopes. When lightning broke over their heads, so that their hair stood on end, there was a wholesale retreat. Joyful singing could be heard on the ramparts above them and some freelances thought that angels had come to defend the town.

Panic was quick to set in as they fled and tumbled down the steep rocky slopes. Many hundreds were killed in the falls.

A crossbowman, a seasoned mercenary, punched his Captain in the face when he tried to stop him showing his back to Aln. He threw down his crossbow, his precious companion with its parchment covering and horn inlay, and crushed it in the mud with his armoured boot. 'I'm not fighting the Anointed One's Kingdom!' he screamed in his Captain's face, and stormed off in the heavy rain.

The forces of The City had not expected to encounter such resistance. Many of the freelances had heard rumours of what was going on behind the walls of this backward town The City was so anxious to destroy. They began to ask each other, why? There was talk of women walking around freely and naked as Eve, no work, no hunger, as many wives as you could catch. There were those who, if they thought it had been possible to keep their lives as well, would have deserted to the Holy City.

'It is not right to have a Temporal City and a Holy City,

and why can't the two exist side by side?' wondered a freelance outside his tent. And there were many who asked the same. As a result of the unhappiness of the men, it was decided by The City to abandon the idea of seizing the town and instead to blockade and bring it to submission through starvation.

Headed by Lumb the Butcher, a joyous procession marched through the town to the Royal Palace, singing hymns of thanksgiving, picking up people as they went. They demanded that the King address them and there was a deafening roar when he appeared on the balcony. His steady eyes calmed them.

'Enjoy your victory, my friends, but do not remain in the unsteady state of rapture for too long. There is worse to come.'

How the King was admired for always responding to every situation with wisdom. No emotion was strong enough to distract him, be it despair or elation. It was impossible to fathom his true intention because he saw so far into the future.

'It is when we slacken, if only briefly, that we invite devils to sup with us. We must remain diligent to the last moment. This is the chosen place where we are safe. It is a bitter and yet inevitable task that we have been entrusted with. I know you are all capable.'

The madness of exultation had been momentarily dampened. 'Enough,' thought Konrad, 'We must lose no time in the repair of the walls, strengthen our gates, our earthworks, otherwise we may find ourselves overtaken...then enjoy yourselves!'

Declining the offer to dine with them in the Square, the King spent the evening assessing the reports of the discussion meetings before retiring early with some of his wives. If the truth be told, many were relieved he had declined their offer. Now they could relax and be themselves. Who could relax in the company of the King? They did not want him to witness the scenes of total drunkenness and debauchery.

The subject given at that night's discussion meeting had been, 'What does it mean to be a patient person? Are you a patient person? Is it a virtue or is it a symptom of impotence?'

37

Julius was still unhappy. He no longer mortified his flesh in secret but, rather, put it through its paces. After he had seen the children to bed following a particularly lively discussion meeting, reported to Konrad, and served him his supper, he retired to his room. He had felt uncomfortable all day, and the humidity didn't help. He knew that Konrad was dissatisfied with him, and that was a torture. 'Why am I such a disappointment ?'. he muttered, overtaken by a sullen heaviness. He went over and over the day's events in his fogged mind, checking each act of service to his master. It must have been the battle, he thought, that made him irritable. But when he had been collecting Konrad's supper from the kitchen he spilt some claret on the tray and had flushed with irritability. It was not the battle or the ensuing siege that was irritating the King, but him. And worse, he knew it was not some physical mishap or oversight that had triggered off the King's coldness towards him. If he could have pinpointed a reason, an incident, he could have staved off his depression. But no, it was for nothing he had done, it was for what he was. And since Julius had no conception of what he was, he could not put it right. Nor would he have the audacity to ask the King what he was doing wrong. Anyway, it wasn't 'what' it just 'was'. In his worst moments he imagined the King had taken him as a disciple because he was the biggest challenge he could find, the most sinful. The King was always choosing the hardest tasks for himself to sharpen his spiritual abilities. There was no reflected glory in the presence of the King, only the intensification of his inadequacy. Then, in his very darkest moments, Julius had imaginary conversations with him in his study where he was refuting the implicit criticism. The conversations never reached a conclusion. Julius was always able to force himself to stop before reaching the inevitable. It always began in the same way. Julius would enter the King's bedchamber, place the breakfast tray on the side table, and say, 'I'm afraid I won't be able to take the Classics Class this morning.'

The King, caught unawares, still vulnerable with sleep, would answer, 'What's that you say, Julius?'

'I will not be teaching this morning. You will have to find a replacement.'

'Are you ill?'

At this point Julius' head would begin to swim, making him sick.

'I am despised.'

The King would not answer. He would stare from under his coverlet, neither denying nor agreeing.

'I will never be adequate, therefore I will never be happy. It is not a question of sentimentality, it is a question of honesty. I must remove myself in order that someone who has the capacity I lack can serve you in the required manner...This is my only way of creating value.'

Usually the fantasy stopped here. If he was outdoors, on the roof, he would run; in private he would bite his tongue until it bled. Lately, he was unable to control his thoughts with this method.

Closing the door to his room, Julius proceeded to prepare for a penance. He dressed in all his shirts, scarves, gloves, hat and overcoats, and dragged two heavy stones from underneath the bed. It was already airless in the attic room on a humid evening. The heat generated inside the clothes made him stagger.

He began by holding his breath for as long as possible. His heart beat like a wren's and his colour changed to scarlet. At first this alone had been adequate, but now he needed to go much further. Picking up the stones, he held them at arm's length. The pain was angry, his heart twitched in his chest so that he could see it move despite the many layers, and the liquid running down his body filled his boots. He fought back the urge to scream a

144

stream of profanities because that would have been a pleasurable release. The strain was to concentrate on the pain not the thrill. Veins throbbed in his temples, pulsing with carnal substances rising from the nether regions, almost unbearable, almost, but not quite.

Dropping the rocks on the bed in disgust, and with tears streaming down his cheeks, he forced his arms to move suddenly from their fixed position.

'It is not enough,' he whispered, 'I must do more...and more.'

38

There was a silence waiting in New Jerusalem. What the townspeople were waiting for had become vague. Waiting for The City army to retreat. Waiting for the oppressive heat to lift. Waiting for the arrival of the Anointed One. Waiting for the End? The heat was overwhelming. The air seemed to crackle and quiver as though preparing to burst into flame. To make matters worse they had to witness the soldiers harvesting their precious olives and wheat, waving and shouting at them from on top of the stacked sheaves. At mealtimes, fewer darted from shadow to shadow to fill the refectories. The taverns were empty. Even the most energetic were listless, even Gammy was not playing with his beloved fountain.

'A man must have time with his thoughts,' Gregor the Candlemaker had told one of the Royal Officers who was going from door to door, 'and the sun's hot enough to dry my blood.'

'We can't be public all the time,' said another. No one would admit to being disheartened for fear of retribution.

Finally, on another Royal Justice day, Mr Farr decreed that solitude was a sin. 'The sin of arrogance is wanting to remove your presence from your fellows, and be where your actions cannot be observed, where your true opinions are disclosed to the few. Solitude is selfish,' declared Mr Farr from under his umbrella, 'solitude is only of value to yourself, and who is anyone to think they are interesting enough to be worth spending time with themselves? Even sexual congress cannot require solitude.'

After the Edict had been ratified by an unenthusiastic cheer, Mr Farr made them chant, 'Solitude is Greed,' and play cards under the lime-trees in the Church Close and throw horseshoes.

All avoided walking the streets at night, and made their visits to the privy brief. Only the most hardened drinkers drank.

'Why do you want to go outside the walls when we have everything here?' said Lumb the Butcher, who was drunk.

'Except food,' said Kitty.

'Life consists of a daily routine, simple mundane tasks. There is beauty in them, and grace...'

'We have a holy King, we live in a Kingdom higher than any other.'

'Meanwhile some bastard from The City is helping himself to my olives!'

Food became plainer on the common tables, while outside the walls the freelances behaved as though they were celebrating a Holy Day rather than waging a war. Sometimes, at dusk, their drunken songs would drift on the wind and if any heads appeared on the ramparts they would see bared bottoms and rude signs and sometimes worse.

'Come and join us,' the freelances would shout and, 'What are you waiting for? We've brewed enough for all!'

Smells of roast ox were the hardest to bear.

Such smells Mr Farr called 'the devil's farts'.

The visions increased - faces in the night, mysterious strangers. A young woman saw a boy wandering alone in the streets. Taking him by the hand, she felt a shock run up her arm, the boy's glance was so piercing that she had to turn away, and heard the words, 'I am come,' but when she looked again there was no boy in the wavy heat.

All these happenings were reported to the King, along with the humble requests for his presence in the Square, if only briefly. Mr Farr relayed the King's apologies, saying he was well and in good spirits, preparing for Isa's Ascension, that they shouldn't worry. The Last Days had come, enjoy them, he would see them soon.

The grain in the storehouse had been depleted alarmingly, the mill only grinding half a day. And people's needs increased, demanding more not less, and more. Groups of partly clothed women, fanatical followers of the King, danced through the streets, calling out to all to confess their sin before it was too late.

'Give! Give! Give! Give!' they sang, their arms outstretched, eyes fixed longingly up at the clouds.

'Isa will provide...Isa will turn the cobbles into bread.'

Food is the greatest treasure. Its abundance makes a man forget that he is an animal. At the beginning of the eighth month the Royal horses were slaughtered, secretly.

At first it was thought to be the tired ravings of an old brain, but after Ginny Gill the Weaver's wife kept measuring it with a stick there could be no doubt - the water in the well was sinking. Either The City was plugging the source - some thought deep in the mountains - or there was to be a drought. This rumour shook the faith of many. Explanations were demanded from the Palace.

'Isa is testing us,' explained Mr Farr, standing beside the empty throne. 'His wish is to push us to the very edge of unbelief and blow us off. Now is the time our faith is forged. Through suffering comes purity. Impurities rise to the surface and float like effluvium in the sewer, but it can be scraped off. Now, in our hunger, is the very moment to deepen conviction and those who do not will spend time eating their fill...eating their fill of others' filth in Hell!'

'Where is the King?'

'The King works tirelessly, day and night, for our Salvation. He makes painstaking preparations.' Mr Farr attempted to sound reassuring, dressed in magnificent sky-blue satin and silver sash.

The hungrier the population grew, the less care they took over their appearance, and the more magnificent seemed the

Royal Household. The contrast grew starker daily. Women no longer braided their hair but let it straggle down, unwashed. No longer sure of a constant water supply, bathing was discouraged. Red cheeks paled and hollowed, eyes dulled, the young grew hunched and shuffled from place to place, hardly able to finish a sentence. Only the fanatical thrived, and received succour from their hunger.

Julius was pleased with himself. Almost daily, he was discovering new and subtle ways to scourge himself, by denying himself a myriad of simple pleasures. While sitting at the Refectory table, a faint smile played on his delicate thin lips. He sat through the meal in exquisite torture, because he had not salted his food. Simple pleasures are extraordinarily important; without them Julius was becoming gradually incorporeal. Since he had been a little boy he had detested unsalted food. Why had he not thought of it before? What a simple way to deny himself! Flagellation was so primitive. Denial was on an entirely different plane.

In his quiet moments, he took great delight in planning further delicious denials. He progressed to denying pepper, milk, sugar, herbs, and cheese. Alternately he experienced agony and liberation from something. His pale skin became translucent, he counted each forkful of food, reducing them by steady degrees, but yet his body felt stronger than ever, his head clear and light.

'It comes,' he whispered continually when alone.

His control of the sensual tongue was made more delicious by the reports of desperate hunger outside the Palace. When informed by the King that he and Mr Farr were the only members of the household who were to be allowed access to the outside, he had feigned resignation, whereas in fact he was elated. He hoped never to leave the Palace again. The outer world seemed smaller than the Palace. Inside was a succession of individual subjective moments, outside was the objective mundane reality, incomplete and diseased. The inner rhythm he had created within himself perfectly matched his daily routine in the Palace, a perfect manifestation of his secret life. Bit by bit he had defeated ordinary chaos. If New Jerusalem was the true Holy City then the Palace was its Holy of Holies, and he was Keeper of the Mysteries that the King expounded. There was no longer daily life. He was transcending the mundane.

Last thing at night, as a final act of denial, he fingered a book that he had taken from the library, that he hungered to read. He made all the usual preparations to read it, trimmed the lamp wick, performed his prayers, turned down the bedcover, then picked up the book, felt its weight, smelt it, and imagined the pleasure its contents would bring him, then placed it back on the table and put out the lamp.

There was to be no more reading, apart from the Holy Book.

There was to be no more pleasure.

39

As the weeks passed, there was no denying it, there was a famine in New Jerusalem. The mill-stone was still. Starvation showed itself in the ashen emaciated faces of the townspeople, and though it was extremely hot still, they complained of the cold.

As though there was nothing more to say, a turgid despair gripped the town. The Bath House was closed and lice were rife. 'You know what they say,' a woman reminded her husband when he complained about her stench, 'Bathing is a prelude to sin!'

'Sin?' he muttered disconsolately, 'there is no sin.'

Rats came out of the mouth of the sewer during the day. Women reported waking in the night to find them nibbling their toes and entangled in their hair. The shutters were permanently drawn at the Royal Palace, and only the King and Mr Farr were privileged with first-hand reports from the outside. Each day Mr Farr set off with his Guard, walking briskly through the streets, eyes and ears open for incidents to report. A woman claimed that the clumps of hair missing from her scalp were caused by an angel picking her up by the hair.

'"Pity you," he said, the angel, "come with me, I'll convey you to Paradise." "No," I said, "and betray my King! - never." I fought and wrestled with him, and he flapped his wings hard, but such was my resistance he let go and I crashed to the ground.'

'"I am in Paradise," I shouted.' It was difficult to understand her speech, it was so slurred with hunger.

'I am in Paradise, Mr Farr,' and she lifted up her skirt and rubbed her genitalia gleefully.

'Undoubtedly,' said Mr Farr, scribbling hurriedly in his report book and walking on briskly. When his circuit of the town was complete he made his way to the foodstore, which was now

151

more heavily guarded than the Palace. This was the duty he disliked most, to witness herds of previously respectable citizens cursing, screaming and begging for scraps. At first he had despised them for their lack of dignity, but felt moved by their sorrow. But now, all he saw was a beast with many open mouths, fearful gaping holes of despair, and felt sick. Some had been his friends, with whom he had once dined and discussed erudite subjects. One morning his cousin, an Apothecary, broke a tooth while trying to eat a cobblestone that he had prised up with his bloodied fingers from the street. He now carried it everywhere.

'Please, Mr Farr,' he begged, 'ask the King to turn the cobbles to bread.'

Mr Farr, flushing, scribbled down his request, or pretended to.

'That's all we need - bread, and there's certainly enough cobbles for all, The City is covered in them.'

Despite his disgust, Mr Farr regarded those who constantly crowded outside the foodstore as having a remnant of dignity. He had nothing but hatred for those who had withdrawn into themselves, the dispirited who sat outside their houses and didn't even look up to see who was passing. These people he regarded as the true no-hopers. They made him angry. Often he had to restrain the impulse to kick some life into them.

One of the very few who neither sat listlessly outside his house nor scrabbled with the others for a peck of corn, was Flaig the Shoemaker. Perhaps because he had been used to a life of frugality for many years; more probably, he was totally unconnected with his environment anyway. In any event, he continued patiently with his remaining orders, which took his mind off the pain of his hunger. As though sensing he had made his last pair of shoes, the King sent Mr Farr with a message for Flaig.

I would be honoured if you could spare the time to come to the Palace to receive an order for a pair of shoes.

Konrad

Flaig unhesitatingly put down his tools and left with Mr Farr.

It took some time to reach the Palace due to Flaig's age and weakness, and although Mr Farr took pains not to show his irritation, he was left with the distinct impression that Flaig could read his every thought. Flaig still exuded a basic dignity, and if he had not been so taciturn Mr Farr would have thought he possessed a holiness.

Under the protection of the Guard, Flaig and Mr Farr were escorted through the crowd of fanatics outside the Palace and into the cool of the cloistered courtyard. The air smelt fresh to Flaig and he breathed it in greedily. He was led through darkened corridors and shown into a room and asked to wait.

On the table was food. There were olives, fresh bread, pickled vegetables and almonds. Flaig eyed the food for some moments, then left through the door he had just entered. It was not his intention to give the fanatics outside a cause to resent him, and he would certainly be robbed of any foodstuffs he tried to smuggle out, they would smell it. There was no point in reminding himself what food tasted like if he was to re-join a famine. When outside the room, Flaig could not remember from what direction he had come. There were doors everywhere, on all sides, like traps. Behind one of them was the King. He shuffled along the corridors, hoping to meet a Royal Attendant who could direct him to the courtyard. A few yards further along and he thought he heard a door opening and closing behind him and the voices of children, but when he manoeuvred himself around they had gone. 'What a strange and wonderful sound,' he thought to himself, 'like the voices of angels.'

He shuffled further down the corridor where he became aware of more voices, not children's voices this time, but women's voices, and laughter, giggling and the splashing of water. Shuffling on, drawn inexorably towards the sounds, Flaig stopped at the door and, placing his hands on his knees, bent down to look through the keyhole. How could he know it, but Flaig was peeping at the King's wives in their bath-house. Nearest to his eye was a woman with pointed breasts soaping the pear-shaped breasts of another, whose fingers fluttered between her thighs. Behind them, others wandered without shame in their nakedness. The only female flesh Flaig had seen was his poor wife's who had been dead for many years. The woman with the pear-shaped breasts reminded him of his wife, her soft belly distended in the early stages of child-bearing. His eyes prickled with moisture as he was reminded of the feel, the peach-like softness of a fecund belly. He remembered his leathery hand feeling the restless kicks of his son. He raised a hand and gripped the door-knob, not that he - yes, he was turning it, but then -

'What is Flaig the Shoemaker doing in the Palace?' asked a flutey child's voice.

Flaig shuffled himself around like an old ox, to see a boy.

'Trying to get in,' he answered when their eyes met, 'what do you think?'

'But you're from the outside, aren't you?'

Flaig didn't think the question worthy of an answer.

'If you'd be so kind as to show me the way, that's where I'll be going now.'

'But why do you want to go back to the Old World?'

'Because I can only make shoes in the Old World.'

'There's no going back once you've crossed over. Outside is fundamentally rotten.'

'So am I.'

'That is true, but nevertheless you wouldn't be here unless the King gave permission. You must be meant to stay.'

'Why?'

'To help create value.'

'Value?'

'The purpose of human existence.'

'Does there have to be a purpose?'

'Of course, everything has a purpose.'

Flaig began to grow annoyed.

'You only make shoes because that is all you expect to do. Everywhere we are, everything we do is always the most perfect action for our happiness. After all, we can't be anywhere else but here, can we?' The boy giggled.

'No,' agreed Flaig.

'There you are, then. You are present now. You cannot go back to the past. Everything you have ever done has been to prepare you for this moment, because it is only in this moment that you can create value. The past isn't valuable to you now, and you can't create future value unless you create it now.'

Flaig felt a strong desire to put his hands around the boy's neck and strangle him slowly.

'You forgot one thing,' he said instead. 'I didn't choose to come here, it was at the King's command.'

'Yes, you did. You chose by being you.'

Flaig grunted, bared his teeth, and shuffled off. The boy skipped after him and, taking his hand, turned him around and led him to the outside.

Julius stared into the empty room where Flaig should have been.

The King was going to be very angry. He would be so angry that he wouldn't say a word, not a word.

Though he was not to blame, Julius took full responsibility on himself. Though he was not to blame, if he had fulfilled his duties in the correct spirit, it would never have happened. There was a margin of error that ran like a crack through everything he did.

And he was right, the King did not say a word. But the next day he took Julius aside and said, 'Ninety-nine is good. But it is not a hundred.'

40

Konrad had discovered the map of the secret passage within days of becoming Mayor of Aln, among the confidential documents in a locked drawer in Mr Flagg the Elder's desk. He had of course suspected the original building to contain such a device because it had been built in the period of the Warring States, but he had not expected to find it so easily.

Divesting himself of his Royal Robes, and donning his black cloth clothes, he peeled back the carpet in his bedroom, prised open the lid and disappeared. Stooping low to avoid the dripping ceiling, he felt his way through the darkness, and re-emerged in the brightest sunshine from behind a laurel bush at the foot of the West Wall. It was a fine day to be out of the Holy City. The moist heat of the past weeks had lifted. He took a deep draught of the breezy air tinged with the musty smell of olive trees, then scrambled down the slope to the cover of the scrub-bushes.

The City's forces were concentrated mainly on the North side. Konrad had decided to take a look at close hand. Within less than half-an-hour he was within a quarter mile of the main camp, close enough to distinguish voices, and what he saw pleased him greatly. The bulk of the army consisted of freelances, content to be drawing payment for a siege of indefinite length, enjoying the camaraderie and licence of camp life. It was the sons of the City who posed the real threat, the Electi's second sons. Most of them would have no real interest in soldiering apart from the sport of it, but they were fanatical defenders of the hierarchy. They were the ones anxious to return to The City, plotting in their tents to end the siege before the weather turned.

Konrad observed the camp, which looked like a Guild

holiday, for over an hour before retracing his steps to the tunnel. When out of sight of the camp, however, and made unawares by thought, he let himself be plainly seen from the road. It was too late to hide and avoid the cart trundling along the West road, so he strode towards it, whistling. As he neared, Konrad could see and smell the cart was laden with large cheeses, no doubt for delivery to the camp. If the Carter indicated that he wanted a chat Konrad would oblige. The Carter slowed his horse and pushed back his battered straw hat.

Konrad nodded a greeting.

'Cheeses for the camp?' he asked.

'Aye, one load every fortnight. Best thing that ever happened to me, this siege.'

'War produces prosperity in its wake.'

'Aye, but not to those poor buggers inside.'

Konrad could detect a glint of recognition in the Carter's eye. Doubtless a description of him was common throughout the Province, or perhaps a dim memory of a chance encounter in the Square.

'Though I'd hardly call this a war, if you don't mind me saying so, Sir.'

'Oh make no mistake, it is a war of ideas, a conflict between civilization and animality. While the freelances get fat on cheese, the local economy grows and the people are ignorant of a righteous battle which they have already lost.'

The Carter threw back his head with a throaty laugh.

'Well blow me, if I'm not minding me own business transporting cheeses on a fine Summer's day, when I don't meet with the renegade they are calling the New Messiah.'

'I have never called myself that, and desire nothing but peace and anonymity.'

'Anon - Ha!, ha, ha, ha, ha, ha, - You're the most famous man in the Province.'

'That is not my doing.'

'So you deny it, do you? Very sensible, if I may say so, because if you'd said you were the Messiah, I wouldn't have believed you, but because you deny it, you probably are him! Ha, ha, ha, ha.'

The Carter fell to his knees in mock reverence, but when he looked up at Konrad, a dark shape carved out of the sunlight, he stopped laughing, and felt a deep silence in him, and a deep joy burst open inside him flooding his whole being.

On his return, Konrad ordered the security of the West Wall to be strengthened, and burned the drawing of the secret passage.

It was some hours later that the cart of the abandoned cheeses was found in the road, and further along, the Carter's twitching body.

41

Julius had decided to let go of the beam. Either he would break both his legs or he would float to the ground. Perhaps in the arms of an angel, or at the very least an invisible protective force would be summoned.

In the event, the experiment did not turn out as expected. After swinging himself from side to side in an attempt to release his fingers, he realized that his fear was producing a titanic strength. He could have stayed up there for hours. When, finally, he let go, not out of trust but failing strength and numbness, he landed on his feet with such a crash that he jarred his whole body terribly, and there was no force to help him, unseen or otherwise, nor any broken bones to nurse. The whole episode was a huge disappointment. After some days pondering on the causes and consequences of his failure, it occurred to Julius that he was still attached to testing the flesh alone. Now that he had adjusted his palate to the plainest possible food, and no longer cared for reading, he needed an ascetic practice that didn't inflict too much harm on the body, leaving tell-tale signs, but tested the spirit and the flesh in equal measure. He was not, after all, attempting to merely tolerate pain or defeat cowardice but doubt in a power outside himself. He hit upon the solution after reading over the King's instructions to a child who had become undisciplined. The King had written, 'True faith is not an intellectual exercise requiring a particular capacity on the part of the individual. Faith can only be said to be genuine when it is manifested in action. After all, is not faith the absence of doubt and the subsequent appearance of evidence? Doubt therefore is a treasure because without it we would be unable to forge out faith. Without doubt we could not believe.'

The boy had cried penitently.

'Do not repress your doubts!' the King had written comfortingly, 'for that is blind faith.'

At that very moment Julius hit upon a plan that would transcend mortification. In short, he devised for himself a perfect test of faith and discipline. This one test alone would, in his mind, prove his faith genuine. Overcoming this last hurdle would make him pure. He was so excited that he could hardly stop himself from feeling emotion.

He began while serving the King his morning tea.

'Sir, I would like permission to take two women into my bed.'

The King, unperturbed at this sudden reversal, took a sip of tea. Relations in the Royal Household had become complicated of late. Because of its virtual isolation from the outside, relationships spilled out over the boundaries of marriage and a network of 'temporary' liaisons were arranged unofficially. The King was aware of what was going on, but had not so far felt the need to intervene; whereas Julius, known for his dislike of coupling, or indeed any sort of bodily contact, had on several occasions reprimanded the Guard and members of staff for their promiscuity and had avoided taking even one wife for himself.

The King leapt out of bed, parted the curtains and peeked through the shutters to the Square below. It was all but deserted. A man danced with himself, an argument between a man and a woman.

'Who do you want?' he asked.

'Sussana and Rachael,' Julius replied.

Rachael, raven-haired, round hips, Sussana's almond-shaped eyes, both married, both very promiscuous.

The King turned to Julius and nodded.

'Whatever you think best, Julius,' he said.

Julius bowed and backed out of the room. He would prove himself to be worthy to serve the King, and perhaps even...

Rachael and Sussana were both very surprised, and delighted at Julius' invitation and spent the rest of the afternoon in the Bath House. Whatever Julius' opinion of his own role in the Household, to the rest of the staff he was the King's adopted son.

A thrill of anticipation coursed through Julius with mounting pressure as he despatched his daily duties with aplomb. He had fixed the appointed hour with the women. After dinner he would have enough time to prepare his room. He requisitioned some silk sheets, a candelabrum, crystal glasses and a triple wine ration.

He hummed as he busied himself with supervising the discussion. How he seemed to love the children even more that night, and how popular he would become when at last he conquered that most terrible and powerful of demons - himself!

At the appointed hour, after the time when most of the fanatics outside the Palace had stopped howling and screeching, Julius was prepared and waiting and the women arrived punctually. Both were heavily perfumed.

'Whatever you want us to do, we will,' said Rachael.

'Anything,' agreed Sussana.

'Good,' said Julius. 'Well, first let's drink a toast to celebrate such a rare occasion, an activity that I hope becomes a regular habit - to perfection!'

'Ah yes, we'll drink to that,' said Rachael, beaming with happiness. The women had never seen Julius so relaxed and animated.

When they had finished the bottle Julius undressed and lay on the bed, propping pillows behind him for comfort.

'Now, both of you undress - but please, very, very slowly.'

Julius watched intently as they peeled away their clothes, his face a mask of concentration, and his member flaccid. When both women were naked, he motioned them to lie on either side of him on the bed, but indicated he did not want to be touched. And so they remained, all night. Eventually Rachael and Sussana fell asleep, then Julius examined their unconscious bodies from many different angles, moving his hands close to their sensitive and secret parts, and never once touching. Julius underwent in this way the greatest ordeal of his life, without drawing a single drop of blood or semen, by preventing his member from stiffening under the greatest provocation. He repeated the exercise many times and with many variations.

42

As winter approached, the besiegers increasingly fired leaflets into the town, offering amnesty and safe conduct to all, if only they would hand over their King and his Court.

'If not, you will be butchered indiscriminately or die from hunger.'

Even if there were some who wanted to act upon these tempting suggestions, they were not able to. The whole population had been rendered hopeless by hunger and the fanatics would have torn to pieces anyone attempting to leave. Only those who had foreseen the siege had been clever enough to hide a little food, dried fruit and olives mostly, and avoid the constant searches.

Knowing that the end was near, many of the army Officers had left for The City, leaving their Captains in charge. A siege was not as honourable as a battle to these men, and knowing what would follow when the walls were breached, thought it best not to be associated too closely. Some of the Officers even secretly hoped the siege would not end, but that a compromise would be agreed, sensing somehow that The City would suffer repercussions beyond the capture of a Pseudo-Messiah. Also there was growing discontent among the mercenaries. The bonhomie of the Summer Camp had vanished with the Summer. They were cold, missed their families, were satiated with pleasure, and realizing that the payments would soon cease, were anxious to break the walls and find out what treasures were inside.

The children of the Court were comfortable and well-fed. Those inside the Palace were largely ignorant of the degradation of the populace. The death-rate had increased twofold. There were scenes in the streets of New Jerusalem, especially at night, that the children could never imagine, even in their nightmares.

A lone figure scuttled through the peasant quarter, dodging from doorway to doorway. His cold damp clothes clung greasily to his emaciated frame. Under his arm he clutched a canvas bag - that twitched. One year ago this man had been a prosperous Butcher, with a wife and a daughter. Now, his daughter was in the Palace, his wife was a handmaiden to the Queen. His teeth were loose, his skin grey and scabbed. He had done many terrible things in order to obtain food.

Inside his house were two men and a woman, waiting for his coded knock. When it came one of the men nearly passed out with excitement. The woman slapped him into silence.

'Did you get them?' she whispered to the Butcher, eyeing the sack.

'Yes,' he replied, holding up his haul.

'How many?'

'Four.'

'Four?' she cried, crestfallen.

'Look, I was lucky to get that many, they're getting scarce. If you're not happy you can risk it yourself next time.'

One of the men shook his head vigorously.

'Sssssssh, stop arguing, you two. He's done well.'

'Give them here,' hissed the woman.

On the stove was waiting a large pot of boiling water. Four plates were set on the table. The woman untied the sack and emptied the contents into the scalding water, slamming down the lid. It didn't last long, but the squealing was surprisingly loud, even with the lid on.

When judging them to be cooked, the woman invited the others to sit at the table, or ordered rather, and forked out the contents of the pot one by one. Instantly, the diners' fingers were busy, peeling back the fur and skin with their teeth, separating the parts.

'Don't waste words thanking me, will you?' barked the Butcher, not taking his eyes off the prize on his plate. Then for no apparent reason, one of the men began to cry, his shoulders twitching up and down, gasping loud sobs that formed into a long wail.

'Shut your mouth,' said the other man without malice.

'What's the matter?' screamed the man, 'I'm eating a rat, that's what's the matter.'

When the cats, mice, and rats gave out, people took to stewing old shoes and the leather bindings of books. Then rope, the bark of trees, paper and moss.

43

When the end came, it was sudden.

Mr Farr read and re-read the leaflets offering amnesty that he smuggled into the Palace. He couldn't get the word amnesty out of his head. When Julius overheard him muttering, 'I don't want to die,' and reported it to the King, he knew the time had come. He escaped at night, just as it started to rain gently, but his disappearance was not discovered until he did not turn up for his duty report.

A Guard was sent out from the Palace to find him, but Mr Farr was well-hidden in a small empty house in the East Wall. Feeling hungry and thirsty, he decided to risk it. He walked boldly to the main gate, with all the dignity he could muster, and told the Guard that he was to deliver a message to the enemy from the King. It was only after bullying and threats that he was able to persuade them. When outside, he fell into a trot, slipping in the mud. It wasn't until he was nearly at the bottom of the hill that he was spotted by a freelance.

At first he was mistaken for the King, because of his health and rich clothes, which secretly flattered him. He was given food and drink, which he refused, much to the Captain's surprise, and questioned as to the situation and conditions in the town, and more importantly, the weakest point of defence. Mr Farr was most forthcoming about the condition of the populace, but tried to conceal his involvement in the Royal Court, and asked for an extremely large sum of money before revealing the least defensible area of the walls. At this point the Captain and his men laughed uproariously and slapped him on the back. But when Mr Farr persisted in his demands the Captain stopped laughing and placed a knife at his throat and a huge gob of spit in his face.

The first troop set off in a terrific thunderstorm, on foot, all expert with the knife and grappling hook. Mr Farr led them to a part of the East Wall where it sloped considerably and so was easy with the use of ropes. At the top was a watchtower that was now hardly manned at night, being on the opposite side from the Army, and because of the paucity of capable men.

When the Captain had assessed the situation, asking Mr Farr a few additional questions on the positioning of buildings, he made a signal to a freelance, who swiftly sliced Mr Farr's throat so that he appeared to have two mouths.

There were four men in the watchtower, all asleep, all slaughtered easily before they could raise the alarm.

The advance troop reached the main gate with little difficulty, following the detailed and accurate map drawn by Mr Farr, and with virtually no resistance. It was only when the main gate was opened and the freelances flooded in with cries and cheers that the Guardhouse was alerted and the alarm bell was rung.

The rain and the darkness compounded the confusion. The King was already at the window when Julius rushed in. They watched together the freelances rushing into every building on the Square and preparing to batter down the doors of the Palace. Julius released a flood of piss on the carpet.

The King took the weeping Julius' hand gently, and said, 'Till we meet in Paradise.'

The door of the children's dormitory opened and the King's silhouette stood in the doorway. One by one the children woke, rubbing their eyes and whispering. They could not read the expression on the King's face. After some moments, without a word, or a sound, the door closed.

The Palace doors were breached. One of the Captains, who had interrogated Mr Farr, anxious to gain fame and promotion, forced his way ahead, through the ante-rooms, ignoring the movable goods that his troops were looting, and entered the apartments of the King. He found the King's wives, all huddled in one bed, so frightened they were soiling themselves. He found the dormitory and chalked a cross on the door, indicating those inside were to be saved. Desperate now, and sensing his quarry was close, he burst into the King's study, just in time to catch a glimpse of the King escaping through a secret door in the wainscoting and locking it behind him.

By the time the Captain had battered his way through the secret door, the King had escaped down a maze of dark corridors. In anger and fury, the Captain returned to the King's wives.

The besieging forces were streaming through the streets. The citizens of Aln fought them with desperate courage, so fiercely that some of the freelances became worried. With no leaders to guide them the citizens attacked the soldiers with any object to hand and hurled missiles down from the upper floors of their houses. They barricaded the Square with waggons and benches and carried most of their guns there. Snipers took position on the roofs and in the towers.

The Captain had not expected such resistance, and in the noise, rain, confusion, had difficulty in grouping his men quickly enough to prevent a vicious battle. The freelances were in any case more interested in goods than in stopping the citizens from forming a hopeless defence. A surprisingly small number of them were surrendering, but the ones who did were killed instantly.

Gradually, however, the superior numbers of The City swept away the barricades and a full-scale massacre ensued. One by one the doors of the towers and upper storeys were battered down and the snipers thrown from the windows and their heads burst open on the cobblestones, or impaled on lances. Soldiers became butchers, blood-splattered and frenzied. The slaughter continued all night, into the dawn, until mid-morning. The sewer-mouth was choked with bodies. It was only when the General arrived with Agents from The City that the freelances could be prevailed upon to stop.

Surveying the scene in silence, the General and the Agents were reminded of the disgusting scenes painted of the Warring States period.

It was also a source of great annoyance to them that the King had still not been found after an extensive search. Each body was examined and then carted out of the town gates to the mass-graves being dug on the plain. In the Church, a makeshift hospital was set up but very soon it ran out of bandages and salves. The City Agents called a meeting in the Council Chamber.

'Soon,' said an Agent, 'Aln will have many visitors. When the trial begins the eyes of the whole Province will be upon us.'

'Sir,' said the General, 'by the end of today, there will not be a single dead body left in Aln.'

'Those still alive must be treated with respect and honour. Give them whatever they want. Please see to it they are nursed back to health. It is the wish of the Electi that the remaining citizens be re-assimilated as soon as possible.'

'It will be done,' said the General.

'But there will be no trial without Konrad...so where is he?'

The General and the Captain shook their heads and mumbled.

'Sir, we have searched. He's simply disappeared.'

'Are you telling me he is no longer in Aln?'

'No, Sir, that is impossible. It is my guess that he is still somewhere in this building, but the place is riddled with hidden rooms and passages. It might be necessary to tear down the whole building to get at him.'

'Mmmmm.' The Agent thought for a moment then said, 'Bring me a fool.'

'A fool, Sir?'

'An idiot, but one that speaks. He's sure to be alive. Just ask one of the townspeople.'

Gammy's name was everyone's reply when the soldiers politely asked where they could find the fool.

Gammy was absolutely delighted to be taken to the Council Chamber and made to sit in a chair before the Agent.

'Now then, Gammy, we would like you to help us. Would you like to help us?'

Gammy nodded.

'Good. Now, Gammy, we are trying to find Mr Konrad, the Schoolmaster who you may remember was the King. Do you know where he is?'

Gammy nodded.

'Very good. So, Gammy, would you like to tell us where he is?'

Gammy shook his head vigorously.

'And why not?'

'Because...if I told you where he is it would be a lie because I don't want you to know, and I cannot tell a lie.'

'Oh, come now, Gammy,' said the Agent, smiling and rising from his seat, 'are you telling me that you won't take us to the man who has destroyed your town? The man who has made your people a laughing stock throughout the Province?'

Gammy shook his head.

'Then will you please take us to him so that we may offer our allegiance?'

'Very well,' said Gammy.

'Kings are always betrayed by an innocent fool, are they not?'

Gammy nodded.

The soldiers fell on Konrad like a pack of dogs, and dragged him from his hiding-place in Gammy's hovel.

'If you can do anything, straw King, free yourself from us,' shouted a soldier in his face.

Tearing the heavy gold chain from his neck, they kicked and punched him unconscious, urinating on him, then bound and dragged him back to the Council Chamber, where he was imprisoned in the kitchens, the dungeon being full of those who had been prominent during his reign.

Four days after the conquest of Aln, Mr Jacob, the Judge and members of the Lesser Electi arrived with their entourage. The General of the Army rode out to meet them before they entered the town gates and formally handed over the gold chain, the Sword of Justice and the keys to the town. The inhabitants of Aln needed very little encouragement to clap and cheer.

After they had inspected the destruction, and chatted sympathetically with the stricken population, they ordered an immediate reconstruction before the trial could commence, and released the funds to do it. Every citizen was to be recompensed for any destruction caused to his home and property by the invading army. Even those who had been members of the so-called Royal Household were reprieved and allowed to remain in Aln. Every citizen was also required to sign a disclaimer that any defence of Konrad's claim to Kingship would result in banishment.

Every single citizen denounced him.

44

Throughout the month that followed The City strengthened its influence on Aln and put their victory to good use. The Electi sent their best Officers and Ministers to indoctrinate the townspeople of the renegade town. In a remarkably short time a sense of order and stability returned. The Civic Reception Hall in the Council Chamber was filled with the sound of hammering as the Carpenters constructed a courtroom large enough for such an important trial. The Civic Hall, formerly used as a refectory by Konrad, was vast, brilliantly illuminated by windows of painted glass, with a high raftered ceiling and massive stone pillars.

At one end would sit Mr Jacob, the High Judge, on a high dais. Beside him would sit the top City Judges. This alone when it was announced caused a considerable stir. Never had Mr Jacob or his best Judges ever left The City. Below them would sit a row of magistrates from the North-Western region, and a row of notaries who, quills constantly poised, would write down every word spoken during the trial. Below them to the left and right would sit the Clerks of the Court and the City Prosecutor, and there was to be a witness stand. There was to be no City Defender since one of the many charges brought against Konrad would be rebellion, thus removing the right to defence from the Province.

Any motions of defence would have to be conducted by the prisoner himself. Also, parting with tradition, the trial was to be conducted in the vernacular.

In the exact centre of the Chamber was the spot marked for Konrad to stand, and, running down the entire length on both sides, Carpenters were busily constructing the raked benches capable of seating many hundreds of people. The best seats at the front were already reserved for the prominent citizens of Aln still alive, who, far from being despised, were now greatly pitied and respected by public opinion and had adopted an air of heroic victims. Whereas immediately after the unfortunate 'incidents' perpetrated by the over-zealously patriotic freelances most of the population denied ever even knowing who Konrad was, now they freely admitted their personal involvement with the tyrant whose reign of terror had precluded any attempt at opposition whatsoever. In fact, personal involvement was being exaggerated since it was announced that those who had suffered personally at the hands of Konrad would receive a substantial pension paid quarterly, and that every child could apply when he came of age. The Electi were bombarded with applications for the pensions, and none were refused.

Meanwhile, investigators were having to throw their nets wider since they still knew virtually nothing about Konrad's history before arriving in Aln. Those considered most likely to know the truth about Konrad were the children, and Julius. Julius was most helpful about Konrad's teachings, but ignorant of his history, and the children - not one child had spoken a single word since The City forces had entered the town, even though they were interviewed by the best investigators for hours on end. Afterwards they had been returned to their parents' homes where it was hoped what was considered their profound state of shock would be smoothed away. They behaved quite normally, were polite and calm, but just would not, or could not write or speak a word. Mr Jacob was very concerned. Parents came to see him stating that they were frightened by their own children, who functioned normally, looked the same, and yet were very different. Though Konrad was not even in Aln his influence was still on them. Mr Jacob decided to intervene, asking for one of the older boys to be brought to him. The boy was asked to sit, which he did obediently, and then he stared at Mr Jacob, showing no apparent unease at being back in the Council Chamber.

'Whatever you learnt from Konrad, you must forget,' said Mr Jacob. 'You have experienced a nightmare, but now the Electi will do their very best to comfort you. You will never want for anything for the rest of your life.'

The boy smiled, then without a single stumble or hesitation, accurately recited the contents of a letter that Mr Jacob had written to his wife which he placed in a sealed envelope in a drawer before the boy had come in. It was quite intimate for a man of his advancing years.

'That will be all,' said Mr Jacob blushing. The boy bowed and left.

The cost of the siege, the trial and the pensions were very detrimental to The City's purse. After discussion by the Electi, a plan was drawn up to re-coup the losses. Konrad was to be toured throughout the Province, from village to village and town, in an iron cage. A charge of two ri was thought to be reasonable to see the prisoner and watch him being tortured. With the many thousands the Electi felt would flock to see the most infamous man in the Province, they might, they considered, clear a little profit.

45

It was already dawn and bitterly cold when the cage wheeled off to another destination further South. When the assignment had been announced the soldiers had clamoured for the job of escorting Konrad in a cage around the furthest regions of the Province. But as the weeks had passed and the cold weather had taken hold they had grown closer to him and the task was growing quite onerous. It was almost a sense that something was out of its rightful place. Now that they were moving to the warmer South their spirits rose a little.

The routine had remained unchanged throughout the tour. Konrad was woken before dawn and given his only meal of the day, not enough to satisfy him, and just enough to prevent him from starving. Then the advance ticket-seller rode ahead on horseback to the village or town where the next display was taking place and where the crowds would be frantic to purchase their tickets. Usually the tickets would all be sold in one go, but in the larger towns more than one - of what the soldiers now regarded as a performance - would have to be arranged. Selling tickets was the most difficult job, when youths ran from village to village trying to pass their old tickets off as new, or with local criminals forging them. For many places it was the most exciting event that had ever taken place in the history of that region.

After the soldiers had washed and eaten, the cage would be hooked up and the procession would set off. Though they had always left before dawn there would always be a few stragglers who followed them, fanatics, who would follow for miles sometimes, calling to Konrad, begging the soldiers to release him. But apart from the rare occasions when they were alone with him in open country, the curtains around the cage were drawn closed, so no one was going to get a free glimpse.

Each of the soldiers had spoken freely with Konrad, a fact the Captain of the Guard chose to ignore. Within the first few days Konrad had earned the respect of them all, because he maintained dignity under provocation.

The reactions of the people encountering the procession was very varied. Once Konrad was pelted with flowers by a group of young women on their way back from Church. Another time, an ancient peasant hobbled after the cage for five miles, crying and throwing coins at the soldiers saying that if they didn't release Konrad the Province was doomed. Then another time, a band of farm boys ambushed them, braying for Konrad's blood, throwing filth from the privy, calling the Guards traitors for keeping him alive. Always Konrad's reaction was the same: he would murmur at some point, 'These are my people.'

On this particular morning, at eleven o'clock, the procession climbed the last hill before seeing down below their first proper Southern village. As they approached the gates the soldiers' gait became more measured. They had through their association with Konrad acquired a remnant of his dignity. It is difficult when accompanying the most infamous man in the Province to not feel a little pride.

A dense crowd had gathered in the village square, the noise was deafening. The Captain was reminded of bees at the entrance of a hive.

A pathway was cleared through the wall of bodies, all a forest of arms waving tickets in the soldiers' faces. Music was blaring, harsh reed pipes and tambourines mixed with the braying of asses. Within the crowd, simultaneously defending and selling their wares, were the salesmen who were attracted to any big event. A man was roasting chestnuts on a charcoal brazier. There were screams of 'Marzipan, almonds, nougat!' but only crowding them were small children trying to steal, taking advantage of the safe anonymity of the crowd. A mixture of roast goat, garlic, wine, and unwashed bodies filled the air and a fine reddish dust churned up from the stamping and shuffling feet covered everyone.

Pushing with great difficulty through the crowd was the village mayor, and behind him the priests, their chanting drowned in the cacophony, mouths opening and closing.

The procession came to a halt. None of the soldiers had ever seen anything like this. They were all City men, all wondering what coarse pleasures they could find themselves that night. With the poise of a conjuror, the Captain moved to the side of the cage while the soldiers set up the brazier and made great show of examining the instruments, all part of the entertainment.

The Captain knew there was no point in trying to subdue the crowd first, but then he also knew the effect the sight of his prisoner would have on them. With little ceremony he pulled the cord and the curtain dropped like a skirt.

Within a second there was utter silence.

The crowd sensed its surprise from the people at the front who could see Konrad close up. Perhaps they expected to see a King with a crown and a sword, so that they could pelt him with offal. What they actually saw was a man with a dignified bearing, bedraggled, naked, save for a cloth around his waist, dirty, unshaven, his flesh covered with sooty burns, bruised and lacerated - and magnificent!

For a brief moment there was perhaps disappointment. Then, remembering who was before them, someone shouted, 'Hail King Konrad!' and the pelting started.

'Hail King Heretic!'

'King Devil!'

The crowd closed around the cage like an angry fist. Within reason, people were allowed to be close to the cage, which had been designed so that Konrad could stand in the middle and be only just out of reach from the longest arm span.

This was the worst part for the soldiers, there was always conflict. The thrusting arms through the bars all but obscured him; sometimes there were knives.

Konrad never retaliated physically or verbally to the abuse spewed over him, though it hurt him more than the torture. When the pincers were glowing white-hot they were applied to the fleshy parts of Konrad's body - waist, under the upper arm, thighs, there were no areas that were not unmarked in some way. There was never any shortage of volunteers from those who craned their necks forward, in order to fill their nostrils with the stench.

That night the soldiers took their turn to wander from tavern to tavern chasing and trying to catch young women with their blue blouses and characteristic red skirts, while two stayed behind with the strong box and Konrad. They danced with the village girls in graceful half-moons that spiralled inward and outward, forward and backwards, eerie in the half-light of the lanterns. The village square was deserted now. The only sound came from behind the curtain of the cage. The soldiers on duty shook their heads and glanced up from the cards. Konrad was humming to himself, picking up the folk-tune he could hear faintly in a tavern in the backstreets.

Konrad went on humming, contented.

46

On the third day of the twelfth month the trial began.

Konrad was charged with rebellion, heresy, murder, corruption, fraud, and vandalism. At nine o'clock the doors were opened and an angry crowd that had gathered in the Square since dawn flooded in, scrambling to claim the best benches near the middle. At ten o'clock, as the clock chimed above them, the Clerk stood up and cried out, 'In Isa's name be silent, for Mr Jacob, Judge and Chief of Justice.'

Mr Jacob was the son of a seaweed gatherer. His character was regarded as unimpeachable, his honour unblemished, a man of infallible judgement, whom many considered to be too worthy to soil himself with even the presence of such a foul canker as Konrad. He wore the heavy black silk cowl of the Chief of Justice trimmed with plain ermine; around his neck was the Chain of Office, which he continually held and played with throughout the trial. A skull cap with flaps that covered his ears emphasized his rather fleshy features and mien of a man haunted by a dream too great, the sadness of a disillusioned idealist.

As he entered all eyes were on this secular saint and all tongues stopped as he delivered his blessing in a surprisingly soft voice.

After taking his seat in an ornately carved oak high-backed chair, he said politely, 'Call the prisoner.'

The Clerk echoed the summons - 'Call the prisoner Konrad,' in a high-pitched rasp. The Court then heard the clanking and tinkling of chains for some time approaching before Konrad appeared at the right end of the Hall. His hands and feet were chained, so that he could only drag himself along the polished flagstones with difficulty. He was led by an iron band around his neck.

At first the Court looked uncomprehendingly, not recognizing Konrad as the ex-King. His hair and beard had grown, making him appear older. A grey grime gave him the appearance of an ancient statue, and the black bruises from the burning and scourging seemed like rotting flesh. He appeared to be very dignified despite the heavy chains. His head was held high. It was not what the crowd had expected; he looked lean and powerful. The silence was broken, as Konrad was approaching the chair, by a coarse voice shouting, mocking and venomously, 'Art thou a King?'

To which Konrad replied, almost inaudibly, 'You have called me so.'

At this an uproar broke out over the benches, insults and demands for his immediate execution, and a hail of small stinging pebbles were thrown at him. Mr Jacob's fellow Judges looked to him for a reaction of the Court, but there was none. Mr Jacob looked thoughtful. He realized it would be some days before the public would be calm enough to listen to the evidence in silence. After a time he nodded to the soldiers who began shuffling in a practiced way towards the benches.

'Silence for Justice! Silence for the charges to be read!' screamed the Clerk.

Konrad's Guard locked the chains of his iron neck band to the back of the chair, and the leg-irons to the base. When the noise of welcome had faded the Clerk got to his feet once more, placed eye-glasses on his nose and read the charges. Though his voice sounded impartial and unvarying, a grimace of disgust pulled at the corners of his mouth. As the charges were read the Prosecutor glanced around at the public benches, smiling and feigning indifference as though they were nothing serious. Konrad's expression remained fixed. He stared ahead at Mr Jacob. When the Clerk had finished, he handed the papers to the Prosecutor and sat down. Mr Jacob then asked, 'Mr Konrad, do you have anything to say in response to the charges brought against you?'

Konrad was silent for a long time, then bowed his head.

'Mr Konrad,' continued the Judge, 'do you understand the charges brought against you? The charge of rebellion against The City requires the right of Public Defender to be withdrawn. You must defend yourself. Do you understand?' Konrad was heard to mumble something that could not be heard above the constant murmur from the benches. Mr Jacob strained forward.

'Mr Konrad, the Court asks that you speak up.'

'I am to be made to speak,' said Konrad obligingly, 'though it is irksome and tedious to me, and I am weary of informing the world of my righteousness.'

'I am very sorry to hear you find these proceedings tedious. Nevertheless, the law requires that you admit or deny that you understand the charges brought against you, and on that basis deliver a plea of guilty or not guilty. If you do not understand, which I cannot believe, they will be explained at great length, which will, I can assure you, be really tedious.'

This caused a ripple of laughter.

'There is silence in Heaven now,' said Konrad, silencing the crowd also, and further inciting the hatred of the public, so much so that the Guard were signalled to place themselves in a defensive position at the front benches.

'Mr Konrad, the trial cannot proceed without your participation. However, if you withhold it, you will be removed and the case held in your absence, for the Court is, due to the severity of the charges, prepared to change the law in this respect.'

'I will not be judged by the ignorant.'

The crowd shouted, 'He mocks you!' But Mr Jacob was not to be intimidated by anyone.

'Oh, will you not?' he asked with real patience, 'and who gave you the right and power to rule Aln and declare yourself its King?'

'By what power do you claim it just to usurp my throne?'

'By the power invested in me by the Electi.'

'And I have been called to leadership by Isa, his cross, and the Prophets and Apostles.'

This caused a roar of rage.

'I would remind you, Mr Konrad, you are accused of the greatest heresy, that of declaring yourself the Messiah, and that this is an earthly Court and I am its Judge and I demand to know - how do you plead?'

During the uproar, Konrad motioned to the Clerk and whispered into his ear. The Clerk then approached Mr Jacob and they spoke at some length. Eventually, after consulting with his fellow Judges, Mr Jacob nodded and the Clerk nodded back at Konrad, then called for silence.

'The Court grants the prisoner's request that each member of the bench will write an answer to a question he poses, before he will agree to answer any more himself. The Chief Justice grants his request in the interests of expediency and the patience of you, the people.'

The Clerk then handed out paper and pens to each of the Judges and Konrad asked his question.

'What is bread?'

This produced gales of scornful laughter from the crowd and anger and exasperation from the Judges. Each wrote his answer quickly and handed them to the Clerk, who read them out.

'First. Bread is a staple food.'

'Second. Bread is a mixture of flour and water.'

'Third. A gift from Isa.'

'Fourth. Dough baked in the oven.'

'Fifth. It depends on what part of the Province you come from.'

'Sixth. A nutritious substance.'

'Seventh. No one can really be sure.'

Turning to the assembly on its left, Konrad said in a clear, powerful voice, 'When they decide what bread is they may be capable of deciding other things, for example, whether I am the Messiah or not. Is it not wrong that they cannot agree among themselves, or define something that they eat every day but are unanimous in charging me with heresy?'

The roar of laughter and anger from the benches was deafening, vibrating the glass of water in Mr Jacob's hand. The stone throwing resumed and the Guard took defensive positions with their pikes. The Prosecutor left his desk, and walking towards Konrad shouted, 'Are you the Messiah?'

'It is up to you to prove that I am not.'

'What did you say?' asked the Prosecutor, horrified.

'I do not plead guilty to any charge or recognize the authority of the Court. Therefore it is your task to prove my guilt.'

Both men smiled at one another for a moment, immobile amongst the raging tempest on either side. Turning on his heel, the Prosecutor reported to Mr Jacob that the prisoner had pleaded not guilty and the Court was dismissed until the following morning.

47

On the fourth day of the twelfth month, at ten o'clock precisely, the Prosecutor began his case.

The Court heard from the investigators first on the history of Konrad before his application for the post of Schoolteacher at Aln. For his own protection, Konrad was wheeled into Court in his cage.

'It was my task,' began an investigator, 'and if I may add a great honour, to investigate Konrad's early life. This proved extremely difficult, due to the peripatetic nature of his youth. However, some interesting facts have emerged. Konrad came to The City as a baby and was adopted by peasants. He received sufficient education to acquire the ability to read and write, but no more. It appears that his later fluency in Greek, Latin and Hebrew was acquired by his own efforts. In short, he is a self-educated man. There are no records of his attending The City University or holding any official post, teaching or otherwise, apart from his period of employment at Aln.'

The assembly received this revelation in silence.

'He began his career as an apprentice to a tailor, but when he attempted to establish a shop on his own he was quickly ruined and forced to flee to another district, leaving behind considerable debts. Not that he was bereft of talent. Possessed as he was with an extraordinary grace and good looks, and an irresistible character, not to mention a powerful eloquence, he quickly found his strength in preaching, and formed a considerable following. He was believed by some of his followers to foretell the future and see visions. Forced through debt to abandon The City, Konrad wandered the countryside, setting himself up as a teacher and everywhere causing disruption and bad feeling with his calls for a new order and idealism. He claimed that Isa had revealed to him that the old hierarchy, being merely the work of man, should be replaced by a new one that would be dictated by Isa himself.'

'It is not the intention of The Court to parade a succession of witnesses who claim knowledge of Konrad during his early years, but to prove that he was not qualified for the post of Schoolmaster in the first place. He is a fraud.'

After thanking the investigator, the Prosecutor asked him, 'Do the records show who was the original parents of Konrad?'

'They do.'

'Please tell us.'

'A Mr and Mrs Flaig, shoemakers of Aln.'

This caused a collective intake of breath. Konrad showed no sign or reaction of any kind.

'Do you mean to say,' the Prosecutor continued, with obvious relish, 'that Konrad was born in Aln to the Flaigs, and that his Mother, distraught at the infidelity of her husband, attempted suicide with the baby Konrad in her arms?'

'That is correct.'

'Unfortunately for her and us, Konrad survived. In her distressed state Mrs Flaig jumped from the East Wall, and so into a heavily wooded area. Had she jumped from the West Wall we would not be here today. Be that as it may, it is the Prosecution's contention that Konrad discovered from his adoptive parents the true nature of his origins and that is the origin of his Messianic reign as straw King of Aln. In short, it was a carefully executed plan to exact revenge on a town that spurned him and which was seen, in some perverse way, to have been responsible for his Mother's demise.'

A handwriting expert was then called by the Prosecutor to give corroborative evidence.

'It is my belief,' said the expert, 'that the references that Konrad presented were in fact written by Konrad himself.'

'Your belief?' asked the Prosecutor.

'I am certain.'

'Thank you.'

48

'Call Mrs Kitty Blanch!' cried the Clerk.

To say that Kitty had a self-satisfied smile on her face would not adequately describe its pomposity and suppressed delight.

'You are owner of The Weavers' Arms?' asked the Prosecutor.

'I am.'

'Would you describe to the Court what happened on the night of the eleventh of the sixth month three years ago.'

'Konrad burnt Mr Skully's hand with a candle.'

'Mr Skully being the Schoolmaster who, some thought, was wrongly dismissed, was replaced by Konrad, and can you describe the circumstances that attended such a terrible act of violence?'

'Certainly, Skully was a good sort, well-loved, but he did like a drink, and against his own wishes, and after repeated warnings, the Burghers were forced to dismiss him, hoping he would recover himself and thereby regain his position. Konrad in the mean time was appointed as caretaker Schoolmaster to give Mr Skully time to sober up.'

'And did he sober up?'

'Yes, he did. It was hard for him, but he was making great progress. When Konrad saw that his rival was getting better he became jealous.'

'Jealous, you say, and what form did this jealousy take?'

'Well, it took the form of malicious lies, rumours about Mr Skully's private life.'

'And was Mr Konrad in a position to know anything about Mr Skully's private life?'

'No, he was not.'

'And what were these lies?'

'He was putting it about that Mr Skully had been dismissed because he had been interfering with children.'

'Interfering? What sort of interfering?'

'Interference of a sexual nature.'

There were cries and moans that filled the hall and open displays of anguish. The rows of children sat impassively. Not then, nor at time during the trial did they show any reaction to what was said. They were still an enigma to the many doctors who were examining them. Whether they were still in shock, or faithful disciples of Konrad, they couldn't tell.

'And do you think there was any basis for these allegations?'

'No, it just proves that Konrad has a sick mind.'

'Where you in a position to know anything about Konrad's mind?'

'Oh, I knew all sorts of things about Konrad's mind. I was put into all sorts of positions by Mr Konrad.'

Sensing a prurient disclosure, the audience quietened.

'Please explain Kitty - if it is not too painful for you.'

Kitty became coy and with mock embarrassment gave the following details.

'Well, it was painful all the time, but anyway, as many of you know, Konrad was a guest at The Weavers' Arms for many months before he became Mayor and...'

'Go on, Kitty, we are not here to judge you.'

'Well, during that time, while he was preaching and teaching these poor children, he was giving me a good seeing to at every available opportunity - I had no peace at all - he would force me to do all sorts of things, he liked variety you see, and he used me in any way he saw fit.'

'Did you not protest and resist?'

'Of course I did,' shouted Kitty, 'but he's very muscular, you know.'

'No further questions, Mrs Blanch...My Lord, having

established the violence and perversity of Konrad's mind and character, the Prosecution posits that he be judged indirectly responsible for Mr Skully's suicide. Mr Skully committed suicide because of the humiliation and bullying he received at the hands of Konrad.'

'We will accept the posit,' said Mr Jacob in a calm voice.

'Thank you, Sir, and now I call upon a witness who will prove that the prisoner was directly responsible for the death of Mr Flagg the Senior, former Mayor of Aln. Call Julius Flagg!'

When Julius entered the hall, Konrad was seen to give an involuntary shudder. Julius strolled past him without a single glance in his direction and with something of an air of pride. He was greatly changed in his appearance as Konrad was in his. Instead of his dour scholarly black cloth he wore a scarlet silk waistcoat, russet jacket and a yellow woollen scarf. His hair was short and well-groomed. His complexion was florid and he had put on a quite considerable amount of bulk and weight; in fact, he was getting fat. He looked every inch the gentleman, having just returned from The City.

'Mr Flagg, you were once a close associate of Mr Konrad's, were you not?'

'To my eternal shame, so I was,' he answered instantly.

'It is not the intention of this Court to single out any individual as more culpable than anyone else, you understand. The past is history, and, with the full support of The City, it is hoped the citizens of Aln will be able to forget the past and create a brighter future.'

'And I promise to spend the rest of my life,' declared Julius histrionically, addressing the whole hall, 'to devote myself to the reconstruction of the town of my birth, where the welfare and prosperity of its citizens is of utmost importance to me. I have made all my mistakes. I intend to repay every one of them by contributing every ounce of my energy to the happiness of others.'

This elicited a warm cheer and a loud round of applause from the assembly. 'Long live the Flaggs!' shouted someone.

As he gave evidence, Julius was careful to avoid looking in the direction of the cage. Konrad, in contrast, did not take his eyes off Julius, and at one point was heard to mumble, and was told to be silent. To Julius, Konrad was already stationed in oblivion. But Konrad could see through the glassy stare, the flashy new exterior, the fixed smile.

'Mr Flagg, what evidence do you present before the Court regarding Konrad's torture of your father?'

'Why, from my father himself.'

'Your father told you what Konrad had done to him?'

'Yes.'

'And what did he say?'

'He told me that Konrad had placed his hands around his neck and lifted him up off the ground.'

'And what was the result of this assault?'

'It induced a fit in my Father. It was common knowledge that he had a serious heart condition. Konrad induced the attack in him, forcing, you could say, my father to kill himself.'

'Are you sure your father told you this himself?'

'Quite sure. He showed me the marks on his neck.'

'Why did you not, or he, report this incident to the Serjeant-at-Arms?'

'Because we were terrified of Konrad, and his malign influence...I don't think the Court fully appreciates the evil effects of this man. Even though he is chained in a cage like an animal, he is not harmless, we are not safe. His power is pervasive, it spreads like a smell. If that same influence were used to effect good then there is no telling how wonderful it would be. As it is, there is no doubt in my mind that Konrad is the Evil One.'

Julius received many shouts of support, even one or two of the Judges nodded.

'That is not for us to decide, Mr Flagg. However, your opinion, based as it is on personal experience, is most highly valued. You may step down.'

The next day Julius told the Court the fiscal, theological and political theories of Konrad in some detail, some of which were highly complex and certainly incomprehensible to the majority of the assembly. It was concluded that they were the ravings of a madman in pursuit of an obscure ideal system.

'It was always his intention to develop beyond the Kingship, and he often stated that he was merely using it as an expedient means.'

'Expedient means, you say?'

'Yes. He called his established reign in Aln "preparation", though it seemed to us an end. To him it was a stage, a "phase" he called it.'

'How many phases did he envisage?'

'Three. It was his contention that we still used an animal system of power that depended on maintaining the weak with the strong, and not on making the weak strong. By becoming the strongest possible, by claiming Kingship of Aln and claiming it was the true New Jerusalem he could introduce all manner of ideas and teachings. People would accept them readily because he had conquered them, removed their choice. The person of the strongest belief he would say, or the person seen to have the strongest belief will be the ruler, and the others will lie down and sleep like cats. When change was assimilated he would move on to the next stage.'

'Which was?'

'For each person to be totally responsible, and capable, of ruling the whole. That is to say, the balance between personal and public, inner and outer, would be perfect and equal, and that in itself would create an enormous energy and produce the next evolution.'

'And what would happen in the third stage?'

'The third stage I know very little about. He wouldn't discuss it openly with me, not in a systematic way. But every now and then I would glean something, when he was relaxed or resting, which wasn't very often. And it was something along the lines of daily life being the highest creative act. That is to say, such was people's balance and self-restraint and ability to control emotion and desire, while not eradicating them rather using them as a kind of power, that acts which violated the dignity of life could not happen and daily life would be a constant source of continuing strength. There would still be suffering, but the suffering would be the fuel for constant change, and be useful. He often said the greatest challenge was to exercise self-restraint. In his opinion the system in the Province was fatally flawed because it didn't take into account this clear aim and because everyone assumed that the Electi knew how to do it.'

'Mr Flagg, I think we get the general picture, now if we can move on -'

'Let him continue,' interrupted Mr Jacob, who had been listening with immense interest to Julius' testimony.

'Certainly, your Honour. I suppose Konrad's ideas would best be illustrated by using an example that he used himself when teaching the children in the evolution seminars.'

'The prisoner taught evolutionary theory to children?'

'Oh yes, Sir, frequently.'

'Continue.'

'As I say, the example he used would suit best. Most of the transcripts of Konrad's teachings were burned by the soldiers when they took the Palace but some fragments remain, and it is one of these that I quote. "Suppose," he writes, "there was a town in some far-off place, beyond the borders of the Province. Its people knew no fear of each other or of any situation, nor was there any self-doubt or uncertainty as to the inherent greatness of human beings, and no one imagined it possible to violate human dignity. In short, a town that existed in a land very different from the one we know. Our town, Aln, you could say, is a crude makeshift attempt to recreate this place, without knowing how it was created in the first place. We did not know, for example, that originally, when someone stole, rather than increasing general security and fitting more locks, they made the thief responsible, through dialogue, because they knew he would continue to steal even if he was imprisoned, because of some inherent ignorance, and the security would have to be ever increased as the ignorance spread and would have to become more and more sophisticated until, because there was so much suspicion, it was assumed everyone was a thief, or a potential one.

'Anyhow, suppose it was discovered that Aln was to become unsafe for a long, but finite period. Naturally, the townspeople would expect the Mayor to evacuate them to this safe far-off place. First, the Mayor would be obliged to prepare the people for the change in climate, terrain and custom, in order that they might adapt to a new environment. Preparations would be detailed and thorough. The Mayor would need to keep a secret record of the inner changes undergone by the townspeople, and entrust it to various individuals, those with the capacity to maintain responsibility above personal gain. Then, suppose that some days before they were about to leave, without warning - the Mayor died. And when the distraught townspeople gathered in the Square, there waiting for them were the various individuals. When the wailing had died down, one of these individuals would read aloud from the Mayor's secret record. It would reveal that - there was nowhere to go. There was therefore no need to escape. That the preparations were in order that they be perfectly happy where they were. We are complete. Our minds and senses are already perfect. Everything we need is here, in Aln.'

The Hall was entirely silent and still. Finally Mr Jacob cleared his throat.

'It is the request of the Court that Mr Flagg write down, to the best of his ability, all stories and teachings that he can remember Konrad espousing in the classroom. They will be carefully studied at The City University.'

'Anything to please your Honour,' said Julius, bowing.

49

The following morning was blustery. Squalls of wind and rain whipped the coats of the townspeople as they hurried across the Square to take their places in the cavernous Hall.

When the cage was wheeled on it was noticed that, at the request of Mr Jacob, Konrad had a length of hessian cloth wrapped around his shoulders. There were murmurs of disapproval, but Mr Jacob ignored them. As the days of the trial had passed Mr Jacob's dignified presence had pacified the baser instincts of the crowd without his having to utter a single cross word. He was due to retire soon after the trial, far sooner than expected, and some years later was to write about the events in Aln in his controversial memoirs. It would be no exaggeration to say that Mr Jacob became obsessed with the enigma of Konrad. His speculations and experience were also invaluable to the debate that raged fiercely among the élite during the period of economic struggle that was to follow. That was when many of Konrad's ideas became most influential and not merely controversial as had previously been the case. Having served The City faithfully to the end of his long and distinguished career, his memory lingered because of his role in the trial of Konrad.

'My Lord, it is impossible to emphasize strongly enough,' began the Prosecutor, 'the weight of guilt resting on the shoulders of Konrad. Apart from the murder of Mr Skully and Mr Flagg the Senior, he also caused the death of countless innocent victims during the siege of Aln and its aftermath. A sad day indeed when he walked through the town gates. With my Lord's permission, I request we move to the charge of heresy.'

Mr Jacob nodded briskly.

'I would wish to take the Court's mind back to the Grand Donation of three years ago. It was on that day that a person unknown placed in the Donation Box not an envelope of honest, hard-earned money, but a red button and a letter. The immensity of such heresy is beyond imagination. It is also impossible to imagine the extent of the incessant torture the prisoner will have to endure for eternity. Be that as it may, we are not, after all, with all due respect to the Court, the final judges. But I can prove beyond doubt that it was Konrad who was the perpetrator of that despicable act.'

The Prosecutor reached into the drawer of his desk and pulled out Konrad's silk vermilion Scholar's gown, and holding it aloft, walked slowly towards Konrad. The brilliant colour of the gown was doubly startling in the gloom. 'Where he acquired this gown, which he had no right to wear, we do not know. It is safe to assume he stole it.'

Putting his hand in his pocket, the Prosecutor took out a red button. Holding it aloft, he announced, 'This is the very button that the heretic put in the Donation Box that was bound for New Jerusalem. This is Konrad's gown. If my Lord will examine the gown it will be found that it has a button missing and that this is the missing button, matching perfectly its size and colour. There is no doubt about it.'

'Next we come to the letter included in the envelope with the button. It has clearly been identified as being in the prisoner's handwriting. Mr Clerk, if you please, will read the said letter?'

The Clerk of the Court stood up and said in a dull voice, 'The axe is laid to the root of the tree.'

'Thank you. There can be no doubt as to the authorship or the sentiment,' said the Prosecutor.

Perhaps it was at that point that Mr Jacob was certain that all was not well. A subtle but unmistakable change had taken place in the minds of the crowd.

The Electi had always understood the importance of

controlling ideas, knowing that it was the thinking of one particular idea that made another more sophisticated one possible, indeed, that one thought led automatically and atavistically to another. That was what had created the Electi, the understanding that ideas were linked like the rungs of a ladder. Knowledge of the rungs of the ladder meant they could understand the meaning of all worldly affairs, interrupt any disaster, man-made or otherwise. The Electi administered Justice, despite knowing full well it was on the lower rung of the ladder of ideas. They did not maintain the authority of Justice for their own sake, but for the people's sake. They understood the basic animal belief in higher powers, of respecting those more powerful and hating those weaker. Konrad incited such hatred because he was claiming power for himself.

At least, that should have been the case. Jacob, famed amongst his colleagues for his intuition and clear head, could not ignore the fact that the trial was out of control. Julius Flagg had been right; even though Konrad was in a cage, and would as a matter of course be condemned to death, he still held the power he had claimed. Mr Jacob knew he was engaged in a single combat of ideas, and the people were sensing it, too. On the first day of the trial such ideas as expressed in Konrad's letter to the Electi would have created an animalistic roar of disgust; now there was near silence.

The people of Aln wanted to consider the unthinkable simply as an idea in itself, traditionally the preserve of the Electi. And Konrad knew it. He had always known it.

Mr Jacob's mind raced with the possibilities as he examined the red button between his fingertips. An outbreak of the plague was always a last resort. The town could be quarantined, but for how long? A great fire? Creating wealth in Aln may have been a great mistake. He even began to wonder whether it would be better to keep Konrad alive. Perhaps they needed more time. At least with Konrad alive there would still be a modicum of control, allowing the exploration of further possibilities. He looked at Konrad, which he realized he had been doing more and more frequently, though he made an effort to disguise it discreetly. He had never been satisfied with the little time he had for personal reflection during the trial. It was too late to spend time with Konrad alone. It was all too rushed, as the Electi had ordered. He needed time to think! 'There is no doubt,' the Prosecutor had said.

The afternoon session began with countless townspeople denouncing Konrad. So many had come forward that Mr Jacob waived the tradition and closed the proceedings without all those who wanted to having had their say.

The trial was all but over, and Mr Jacob had many doubts.

50

The day of sentencing was cold but bright, with a frosty sun. Shafts of sunlight pierced the gloom of the Hall, catching Konrad with filtering blues, reds and purples. Everyone had seemed to enjoy the trial so much that there was an air of sadness now that it was drawing to a close. There was no need for more evidence. The Prisoner was proved to be an heretical, murdering fraud. The Prisoner had pleaded not guilty but had offered no defence. He should therefore have been hung, drawn and quartered, and the pieces of him nailed to the gates at the four quarters of the town. That he was to be executed was a foregone conclusion; the verdict was unanimous. However, the manner in which the execution should be carried out was debated at some length: should he be starved first, subjected to the rat torture and so forth? Mr Jacob had very definite views, and in the end his word was final.

Mr Jacob rose to address the Assembly.

'Ladies and Gentlemen of Aln, we have lived through an historical period the like of which we will never witness again. In passing sentence, it is my sincerest wish that normality and sense reign in Aln for eternity, and there be no more talk of Kings.'

It was at this point that Mr Jacob would have expected some show of general agreement, but there was only silence. The atmosphere in the hall was decidedly odd.

'Let us greet the future and consign the past to the dream of oblivion. Due to the surprising evidence provided of the Prisoner's birth in Aln, it has been decided to execute him in the manner traditional to Aln. The prisoner will be thrown from the town walls and his body dashed on the ground.'

This announcement was greeted with polite enthusiasm by

some, but there was no hiding the loud groans from others. The Judges were not happy.

'The Prisoner is advised to beg for the mercy of the Anointed One and prepare himself to burn in Hell for the crimes he has committed. The sentence to be carried out at midday tomorrow. Does the Prisoner have anything to say?'

'I do,' said Konrad at once, his voice surprisingly clear considering he hadn't spoken for weeks.

'The Prisoner will keep his remarks brief,' said Mr Jacob.

'Having listened to the convoluted meandering lies of the Prosecutor, I wish the same remark had been made to him on the first day!'

This drew giggles from the benches, admiration for his humour in dire circumstances.

'Continue.'

'The public and the private are always in conflict, are they not? Inside me is a private world which you have laid siege to as you did to Aln. But my true life is within this dwelling place, my body, for what is the body but the receptacle, the vessel, for carnal substances and digestive juices? It is an enclosure and I attach little or no importance to it. The interior is where my Kingdom lies. And my Kingdom contains many towns, a City, and gardens. In fact, my interior is so vast that I may wander around it for many years and never visit the same place twice. My interior is a vast hierarchy of spaces, it is a Province which has its borders sealed from outsiders because only I may inhabit it, and from which I send messages to you. You cannot invade my Province, because you do not know where it is. It cannot be found or captured. I have tried to tell you truth but you could not believe me. People of Aln, knowing I will die tomorrow I will try once more. Ask your new leaders, "Where is New Jerusalem?", "Show me drawings of its streets", "Let me meet with one of its inhabitants", "Where exactly".'

'Enough!' cried Mr Jacob, calling for the Guard to remove the Prisoner.

'There is no New Jerusalem!' boomed Konrad.

The Guard managed to bang the doors shut and bar them before the crowd broke through to the Judges' bench. Confusion once more prevailed, many fainted, some were angry, some stared ahead, some cried, 'Save me Konrad.'

Konrad sat down at the bottom of his cage.

The sky on the ninth day of the twelfth month, the day of the execution, was slate-grey. Light snow flurries swirled around the Square. The Church bell, tolling since dawn, slowly and mournfully, became almost unbearable. The atmosphere in the narrow streets of Aln was one of infinite sadness. At eleven o'clock the doors of the Church opened and the priests emerged from the darkness in funeral cowls holding large, lit candles. Behind them walked Mr Jacob and the Judges. All walked behind a tall black crucifix. They would normally have been reciting the seven penitential songs, but due to the severity of the Prisoner's crimes they were withheld.

The procession circled the town walls making its way to the Square, which was crammed full of citizens and specially invited guests from The City. The Prisoner was brought out of the Council Chamber under armed Guard. He wore the simple black clothes he had arrived in Aln with. His head was shaved. Seeing him as they remembered him brought a tumult of emotions from within every citizen. Konrad seemed very calm, peaceful even. His eyes were as bright as ever, brighter. Despite all the ill-treatment he still seemed as strong as a bull. His hands were tied behind his back and when he was offered the hood he refused.

Konrad nodded at various people he recognized, and not all the faces turned away.

The children were in the Schoolhouse with the new Schoolmaster.

Konrad's last words were, 'I have nothing more to do here. I go back from whence I came.'

It was not necessary for the soldiers to take hold of him and throw him off the wall. He stepped nimbly up the steps and disappeared in one moment. There was no sound. Some of those close enough were disappointed in their hearts that he had not floated in the air.

Almost immediately after the execution, Mr Jacob and his entourage made preparations to return to The City. At a meeting convened in the Council Chamber it was agreed that Aln would need to be kept under constant surveillance. An official history was already in progress. Relics from New Jerusalem were distributed as gifts to the leading citizens, and certain suggestions made. Konrad's cage was hung from the tower of the Council Chamber.

Gammy was thrilled when Julius and his friends came to visit him.

He apologized repeatedly for the humbleness of his house and not having enough food for them, but they didn't seem to mind.

'Mmmm, Jerusalem artichokes,' said Julius, helping himself.

They practically insisted Gammy join them in the Council Chamber.

When he arrived he saw others there who also seemed very glad to see him, shaking his head and slapping him on the back. When they were all seated and each had been served tea, Julius said, 'Gammy, after a great deal of careful consideration about who should be appointed as new Mayor of Aln, we all agreed that there was only one person who could possibly fit all the requirements necessary to do the job properly....what do you say?'

At first Gammy couldn't say anything. He just craned his neck forward and opened and shut his mouth and eyes.

'After all, it was you who led the troops to Konrad and saved the town.'

How Julius had changed! His hollow cheeks were fleshed

out and rosy; his square chin had disappeared into the flesh of his neck.

'I-I-I-,' Gammy just couldn't explain what he felt, thoughts choking his throat. He began to cry.

'Excellent!' said Julius.

Before he knew it there was wine flowing and he was gulping from his glass and drinking more than he had ever drunk before. Then there were papers placed on the table in front of him, and Julius put a pen in his hand, telling him that he could keep it after making his mark.

Later that night, when Julius and all his friends were very drunk, Gammy started singing, 'I love Konrad, I love Konrad.' Everyone thought that was very funny and had tears running down their cheeks.

Gammy was appointed Mayor of Aln for the rest of his natural life.

On the day that Gammy was inaugurated as Mayor there was a public holiday.

The next morning parents woke up to find all the children had gone. Not one child was to be found in Aln. Even the babies had disappeared.

Fearing the worst, Julius ordered the sewers to be searched, then the foot of the town walls, but there was no sign of them whatsoever.

After it had been established they were not in or around Aln, Julius organized a search-party to travel along the four roads and question anyone they met on the way. This also produced no results. They had simply vanished without trace, and what's more, they were never to be seen in Aln again. Though, months later, there were stories circulating of children missing from farms and villages in the North-Western region, and sightings of a large army of children marching towards the coast, and a tall thin man, dressed in black, leading them. Stories they may have been, but there are some facts.

The night the children disappeared from Aln, a huge amount of money was stolen from the Treasurer's office.

Konrad's remains were never recovered. They had, it was explained, been stolen by souvenir hunters.

A great number of children did indeed go missing from farms and villages at around the same time, and in areas where the reported army of children would have passed through as they were en route to the coast.

A shepherd who had seen a great mass of children joyfully marching and singing asked one of them where they were going, and the reply was reported as, 'To build New Jerusalem.'

City Agents did speak to sailors who had reputedly been offered large sums of money to take a ship of children across the sea, by a man dressed in black.

Whatever the truth, no one knows for certain.